SAINT CODE
THE LOST

A LUCKY DEVIL NOVEL

MEGAN MACKIE

4 Horsemen
Publications, Inc.

Saint Code: The Lost
Book 1 of Saint Code
Copyright © 2023 Megan Mackie. All rights reserved.

4 Horsemen
Publications, Inc.

4 Horsemen Publications, Inc.
1497 Main St. Suite 169
Dunedin, FL 34698
4horsemenpublications.com
info@4horsemenpublications.com

Cover by J. Caleb Clark
Typesetting by S. Wilder
Editors: Jamie Garner and Jen Paquette

Library of Congress Control Number: 2022949010

Paperback ISBN-13: 979-8-8232-0131-5
Hardcover ISBN-13: 979-8-8232-0132-2
Audiobook ISBN-13: 979-8-8232-0129-2
Ebook ISBN-13: 979-8-8232-0130-8

To Betty, the inspiration

TABLE OF CONTENTS

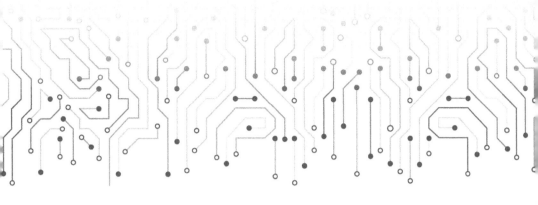

ACKNOWLEDGMENT

Thank you first and foremost to my mother, Connie, for my entire life in general and for proofreading my book three times specifically.

Thank you to Jamie, my editor, who always has my back

Thank you to Caleb for being the standard of talented professionalism.

Thank you to my husband and friend, Paul, for supporting me unwaveringly. I love you with all my heart. Thank you to Byron and Alaina for keeping me motivated.

Thank you to Val and Erika, who reached out their hands and asked, "We're starting a revolution, do you want to come?"

"If you look for the light,
you will often find it.
If you look for the dark,
it is all you will ever see."
--unknown

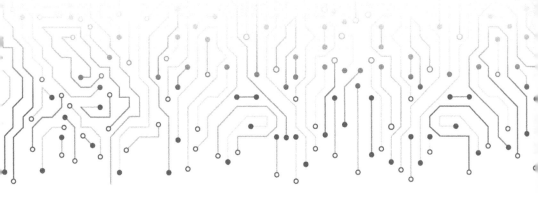

CHAPTER I

In a dark and lonely diner, on the upper reaches of the Data Bowl, an even lonelier woman sat drinking her cooling synth-coffee. Staring down at her hazelnut-colored skin wrapped around the stained porcelain cup, she contemplated the hazelnut creamer she had just added, watching the swirls change from rich darkness to light warm tones the color of her skin. She had simply wanted something that didn't smack her tongue as purely artificial but decided to look no deeper than the hazelnut flavor the hazelnut creamer was supposed to give her drink. Not that she had ever tasted a real hazelnut. Unfortunately, even as she imbibed a swallow, the drink still tasted unreal.

At least the caffeine, and whatever other drugs they put in to enhance moods, still worked all the same. Staring out the window, she considered the darker world outside the diner, dwelling on the beauty of the city beyond. A contrast of continually moving light forming and reforming advertisements amidst the darkness full of distant sounds. The only time it fell quiet and still was during the day. Sometime between nine and eleven in the morning, when the sun beat down from above, the city didn't want to see its drab, broken-down self, so the majority of its residents hid their heads and slept. The first round started to wake at three when the sun had passed its zenith and descended toward the distant, but extremely tall, mountain peaks, until it sank out of sight by five in the evening. Then the city woke itself for another night.

Right now, it was 10:30 p.m., and her client was late.

That figured.

Nothing else to do about that but study the city, read the flashing advertisements one more time, wondering if it would be worth splurging on some water for a shower. She had had the same hair braids forever, and it was very much a hot mess. If this job paid well enough, she might even barter for some argon oil and get some cornrows. Do it all right.

The auto-waitress passed by her table again, carrying a fresh pot of synth-coffee on the end of its mechanical arm. While the squat round thing looked nothing like a human, someone tried to humanize it a little by putting a tiny, red waitress hat on the top of its main body and taped a small matching apron to its front.

It made a motion to refill her cup, but she waved it away. Fortunately, this thing's sensors worked, and it responded to the movement.

"CAN I GET YOU ANYTHING ELSE?" it asked in a digital voice.

"I ordered soup."

"I WILL CHECK," and it zipped away along its glowing track toward the kitchen, stopping to check for synth-coffee refills on its way. There were about a half-dozen or so other patrons seated in booths along the curve of the kidney bean-shaped diner's outer wall. Three other solo patrons had claimed real estate at the counter in front of their own auto-waitress, which roved back and forth dressed in a green hat and apron. Everyone was lost in their own world, oblivious to everything, including the woman observing them.

She could spend as much time studying the room as she did the city and see about as much. Neon lit the space, glowing around the edges of the booths and along the wall, giving just enough light and plenty of atmosphere. Many of the patrons were also decked out in fashionable neon-like accessories around their wrists and necks. Some even had it sewn into their clothes. The room was a reflection pool of the city. Or something poetic like that.

Contrary to the current fashion trends, the woman waiting wore dark clothes. Combat canvas pants with waterproof pockets that hugged close to her body and a close-fitting vest. Practical. Ready for the job. Her long trench coat hung on a hook at the end of her booth. Its only nod to fashion was the blue-light edging at the collar and hem, both of which were turned off when she wasn't wearing it. The cyber goggles she usually wore sat on the table next to her cup, so she could observe the world with her real eyes. Otherwise, anything else she needed lay deep beneath her skin. She could be completely naked and yet not unarmed.

The old-fashioned bell attached to the door chimed, drawing her attention. A woman walked in, dressed in neon orange from head to toe. Her skin was a darker shade than the waiting woman's own, rich as umber. The colors she wore made her skin glow ethereally, which was probably the effect she

was going for. She had dreads piled on top of her head in a bun, with strands of orange LEDs woven throughout, giving her a halo of her own light.

The newcomer made eye contact with the waiting woman and smiled knowingly.

At last, it looked like her client had arrived.

The client sauntered over, her hips sashaying as she walked, her higher-class self standing out in this lower-class world, drawing the eyes of a few of the other patrons as she passed. Once she got to the empty side of the booth, she stopped.

"May I sit?" she asked, like this was a rendezvous and not a business meeting. Which was the last thing the waiting woman needed.

"Depends. Are you the Orange Lady?"

"That depends. Are you *the* Saint Augustina?" The Orange Lady grinned, obviously enjoying the game.

"You've got the right table," *the* Saint agreed, shifting back in her seat.

"Funny. You don't look like how I expected."

"What did you expect?" St. Augustina asked coolly.

"I don't know. I suppose I should keep an open mind," she said wryly as she passed an amused glance around the room.

St. Augustina *did* have time for this, but that didn't mean she actually wanted to entertain the woman's little espionage game. "Are we doing this deal or not?"

The Orange Lady arched her laser-perfect eyebrows, then slid into the booth across from the Saint.

The auto-waitress reappeared, setting the bowl of soup down in front of St. Augustina. "Sorry, I ordered," she said, now feeling uncouth.

"Is that all you want?" her potential client asked, cocking her head to the side.

"Are you going to order?" the Saint returned coldly.

"Indeed." And the potential client passed her hand over the auto-waitress. It glowed briefly.

"UNLIMITED ACCESS," the auto-waitress stated in a slightly different modular voice, before returning to its normal mode. "What would you like?"

"Chocolate cream pie and a cup of tea, please. Then, anything else she would like," the Orange Lady said, gesturing with an elegant hand toward the Saint.

St. Augustina stared for a moment, then turned to the auto-waitress. "A bacon bleu cheese burger and seasoned sweet potato fries."

"PROTEIN BURGER OKAY? WE DON'T HAVE REAL BEEF," the auto-waitress reported.

"I didn't expect you would."

The auto-waitress paused a moment more, then beeped in confirmation. "DOES THAT COMPLETE YOUR ORDER?"

"Yes, thank you," the Orange Lady said sweetly, and the auto-waitress zipped away to the kitchen.

Focusing on her soup, St. Augustina picked up her spoon and began stirring the brownish broth. There were token bits of vegetable in it, but very little else. Most of the nutrition was in the broth itself. The protein burger, which was made of mostly plants and engineered to look like meat, would do more to up her calorie count and go further if this job involved physical exertion. She was starting to have less hope for this meeting turning into something profitable, so if all she was going to get out of this was the first decent meal she'd had in a while, she had better capitalize on it.

"You were vague in your communication," St. Augustina stated.

"Yes. Well, the job itself isn't very simple."

"That's not a problem," St. Augustina said, ladling a spoonful of soup into her mouth.

"You say that," the Orange Lady hedged. "I need you to take a personal journey."

That stopped the next spoonful midway up to the Saint's mouth. "Excuse me?"

"I've been searching for you for a long time. I had to get outside help to locate *you*." The Orange Lady clasped her hands into a pair of pointers that she used to indicate St. Augustina on the word 'you' before bringing them back up to her amused lips.

St. Augustina set her spoon down and sat back, running a passive program and scanning the room again. She did it when she first entered the diner as standard protocol, but this time she checked for anyone showing interest in their conversation. She set it to search for three seconds of attention or more to be safe, all without her client realizing what she'd done. "Do I know you?"

The Orange Lady didn't look nearly as old as she sounded. In fact, calling her a woman was probably generous. Her aura and demeanor were too excited, she could barely sit still. Altogether, she seemed more like she should still be in junior high, and someone needed to phone her mother. At that thought, St. Augustina grasped the small, silver box around her throat on its titanium chain. Sometimes it was the only thing that felt truly real in this world. The contents clinked gently against the sides as the box shifted into the sweet spot of her palm. The Orange Lady's expression remained the same, but her eyes shifted briefly to take in the gesture, before returning to the Saint's face.

St. Augustina cursed herself for giving her a tell. This conversation was already plenty weird.

"We have never met before," the Orange Lady confirmed. "I have heard of your work."

St. Augustina would have gotten up and walked out, but the auto-waitress returned, setting two plates in front of each of them. Something about

this deal felt really off, and really off could lead to really dead. But the smell of beef-simile? Her mouth watered so badly, she had to swallow.

"I'm not saying I'm accepting the job; this is just a business meeting," she said and picked up a seasoned sweet potato fry to stick in her mouth.

"No ketchup?" the Orange Lady asked, cocking her head to the side.

Saying nothing, the Saint chewed deliberately. God, she hated these games. It seemed like everyone who hired someone from the underbelly of society expected it to be all smoke and mirrors and spy thriller. All St. Augustina wanted was for them to get to the damn point.

Instead, her potential patron grinned at her chocolate cream pie as if it was the most delightful thing in the room.

"What is the job, *exactly*?" St. Augustina repeated, forcing patience.

"It's real easy. I need you to do three tasks. You'll be compensated for each one as you have finished it. I need the first task done tonight."

St. Augustina narrowed her eyes, then picked up her burger. "And what's the pay?"

"A hundred thousand credits." If St. Augustina had taken a bite, she would have choked. She hated to be seen as a person who valued money like that, but still, it was a lot of money.

"Per job," the Orange Lady added.

"That's too much," St. Augustina said.

That wiped the smug smile off the teeny-bopper's face. "Excuse me?"

"You're offering me an incredible, too-good-to-be-true, can't-walk-away-from amount of money. Which means," St. Augustina held up a finger, "either the job is incredibly dangerous or," a second finger popped up, "it's a trap, and you don't expect to pay out. Since you were looking for me specifically, I'm leaning more toward the latter."

She took a hefty bite of her burger, juices running down her chin. Damn, it tasted so good.

Enjoying both the burger and the teeny-bopper's discomfort, St. Augustina was in no hurry to leave now, even if she was ninety percent sure she wasn't taking this job. It had stupid written all over it.

"That was the amount I was told to offer you," the Orange Lady said, nearly whining.

"By whom?"

She pursed her orange-painted lips again and sighed huffily. "I can't really say."

"Okay, then. Thank you for the meal, but I'm going to have to say 'no.'" St. Augustina took another bite.

"Wait! Don't you want to hear more about the job first?" the Orange Lady asked desperately, even going so far as to put her hands out to stop the Saint from leaving. Which was silly because St. Augustina hadn't moved a muscle.

"I think this meeting is over. I suggest you get your pie to go because I'm going to keep sitting here and finish my meal like a civilized person. It would be awkward for us both if you stayed," St. Augustina said and then took another bite with delight.

"But... but..." the Orange Lady stuttered, completely disarmed. The Saint continued to ignore her and eat. Finally, after a few awkward moments, the teeny-bopper quietly got up and left, leaving behind her untouched chocolate pie.

A meal and a free slice of pie. Guess the night wasn't a total loss after all.

A familiar chuckle stopped St. Augustina in mid-chew.

"I told them it wouldn't work." Like gravity's pull, St. Augustina turned her head just enough to see *him* sitting at the counter. The pain-in-the-ass's grin grew wider as he took in her response to his presence. "You must be getting rusty, St. Augustina. You didn't notice me enter."

Apparently, her passive scan program needed recoding.

"I noticed," she lied, wondering how satisfying it would be to slip her R-pistol from its holster and let off a shot between his smug, glowing blue eyes.

The other cyborg was dressed all in dark like she was, but instead of neon-lining on any of his clothes, his call to fashion seemed to take him to another era entirely. While his clothing was combat-ready and tight against his lean, strong frame, the fedora sitting atop his head had no practical purpose. Both of his long legs were stretched straight out from his body as he leaned against the counter, his wrists limp. Nothing about his posture said that he was in a hurry or at all alert to danger. His posture was a complete and utter lie. Otherwise, why would he have his augmented eyes glowing inhumanly blue with no sign of iris or pupil within?

Most people didn't realize what it meant for a Saint's eyes to be that way; many normal people paid for cosmetic augmentations that did the same thing in the name of fashion. But there was nothing fashionable about a Saint's glowing eyes. St. Augustina hated them, which was why she rarely activated the augmentation herself. She felt inhuman enough as it was.

"What do you want, St. Benedict?" she asked, picking up a fry to bite it too hard.

"Ha, you just won me twenty credits. Our employer was certain you would shoot me on sight."

"I thought about it."

"I know you did," he said. He seemed to take that as an invitation because the other Saint levered up on his stretched-out legs and swaggered over to the booth to sit in the spot the teeny-bopper had vacated only moments before.

"That's mine," St. Augustina said, as he began to turn the plate holding the chocolate pie so the point was directed at himself. He stopped, then side nodded his head as he turned the point toward her instead. After yielding the territory on the table, he raised a hand in the universal sign for 'attention, I need service.'

CHAPTER 1

"WHAT CAN I GET YOU?" the auto-waitress asked as it slid up to the table.

"Man, what you are eating smells divine," St. Benedict said to St. Augustina, leaning forward to ogle her plate. "I'll have what she's having."

The auto-waitress chirped a moment as it struggled to process the request before it popped a little puff of smoke and zipped off.

"Oh, man," St. Benedict said, waving his hand in front of his face. "That's the equivalent of a robo-fart." Then he laughed at his own amusement.

"I'm not taking any jobs that involve you," St. Augustina stated, not at all amused.

"You better watch out, St. Auggie. I'll get you to laugh before this conversation is over," he replied.

"Don't threaten me," she answered.

"I never threaten. I always tell you I'm going to betray you right up front, and today I'm here to keep you from making the biggest mistake of your life." He grinned over his folded arms before whispering, "So big."

"After everything you've done to me, you expect me to ... what, exactly?"

He resettled himself on his side of the table, folding his hands in front of him, like a missionary gearing up to tell her the "good news."

"The first job is simple. A data fetch. Easiest hundred thousand credits you will ever make."

"I'm not a hacker, and you know that," she said, successfully slapping his sneaky left hand away from one of her fries.

"Exactly, the hacking bit's my part of the job. You're my protection when the system comes after me. Major security where we're going. Nothing you can't handle. And I can guarantee you will enjoy handling it." He rubbed his gloved fingers together to make the cracking sound that leather always made as he continued to eye her fries, at least as far as she could tell without any irises. His own plate of food was coming, but they obviously wouldn't taste as good as hers. Dammit, he was such a child.

"What system?" she asked, trying to keep his focus where she wanted it. They were her fries, dammit, and she would draw blood to defend them today.

"Core Processing."

She rolled her eyes. "Shocker," she said dryly. "Of course you'd be involved in a suicide run. The money is exactly what I said it was: a lie. They don't expect to pay it."

"Oh, they'll pay it. I can guarantee that," St. Benedict said. "And it's not suicidal if it's you and me. We can survive anything together, right?"

St. Augustina's head dropped again with a huff of menace. "Really?"

"The dream team as it t'were."

Why did she like things even less when they made sense? Probably because they became harder to say no to. "That's why they were looking for me specifically. You gave them my name. Did you give them my stats too?"

"They know what they need to know about you. They are more interested in accessing Core Processing's system and are willing to pay for quality to make it happen. I know we can do it. It would be our biggest score ever. Legendary, in fact. We'd finally be queens of this town."

"Queens?" St. Augustina raised an eyebrow.

"Hey, there's two of you, including our representative patron the Orange Lady, and one of me. Seems only fair," St. Benedict said, his eyes twinkling as he shrugged. And dammit if she didn't smile back. No matter how hard she bit her lip, the smile creasing her features even as her teeth tried to pin it down. Which made them both giggle.

He had the unusual grace not to crow his victory. Instead, after the giggles died down, his eyes sobered.

"Let me do this for you. St. Augustina. We both know I owe you. Let this be ... a piece of what I owe you finally paid back."

She knew what he referred to. As Saints, they had been on opposite teams more than once, even though they were trained and modified together from the same school. They had bled, suffered, and yes, even laughed together. St. Benedict had been the one to first make her believe that she would survive the hell that the Deacons put them through. No true religion, the title their handlers, teachers, and torturers had always seemed like a cruel joke that no one even knew the punchline to. The process of modifying their bodies, then training their minds to be the perfect cyberspies, had killed many. So many who never got the Saint title attached to the name assigned to them. Even Augustina wasn't her real name, but she had been altered so far from who she had once been, she didn't even dare think of herself by that name again.

She didn't know St. Benedict's real name either, but she had theories about his previous life. He had been a programmer, someone with talent and the skills to make the most of it. He had been cocky. Hell, he still *was* cocky, but that cockiness had gotten him into trouble then. Now, it pretty much kept him alive. Every Saint was once someone who had committed a crime, or at least what the corporations deemed a crime, and had been removed from society. Whatever requisite skills the Deacons had been looking for was filtered into the Saint program.

All except St. Augustina.

She had just been a black girl taken off the street, never to be heard from again. Girls like her disappeared all the time, and society didn't care enough to do much to find her. St. Augustina wanted to believe in her heart that her parents hadn't given up, but it was just as likely that her father, at least, was dead now. The cancer he had been fighting had come back right before she had been taken. She had no way of knowing for sure, though. They were definitely far, far away from this city. Worlds away...

St. Augustina furrowed her brows, then rubbed her temples.

"You alright?" St. Benedict's soothing voice cut into her painful thoughts. Somewhere off in the distance, she thought she heard a whinny, like a horse, but it was probably just a cat in the alley.

She dropped her head and opened her eyes. What had she been thinking? There had been something not right about it. Something off. Something to do with the city where her parents lived, but she couldn't recapture the thought. It had winked out.

Ignoring St. Benedict's question, she looked back out the diner window at the city beyond, its small lights and neon, the one constant in her life. She clung to their truth.

"And how does all this play into *your* mission?" she asked, giving him a smile laced with acid, the words bitter in her mouth and still a delight to say. As much as he had given her hope to live, he had also been the first to betray her, laying the foundation for their relationship ever since. *His* mission. The one he kept from the Deacons. The one that had nothing to do with the expectations of his employers. The one she had almost died for.

She expected him to turn cold, go still, narrow his blank blue eyes, or wipe the smile off his face. Instead, the artificial light faded from his eyes. Warm, bright irises and a beautiful shade of green-blue reappeared in his face, shifting to almost black in the glowing lights of the booth. They were like the eyes of a demon, staring deep into her soul. It was hypnotizing and disconcerting at the same time, but not threatening. Just sad and happy at the same time.

"This job does involve something I need for my mission," he said, before giving a small smile, the first genuine smile St. Augustina had seen in a long, long time.

"And the first chance you get, you'll dump me if it serves your purposes. I'm a fool to work with you if I have a choice," she informed him. He didn't respond to that, and she couldn't resist plucking at another scar. "You still believe she's alive out there?"

They both knew who "she" was. He never shared her name and had only really talked about her the one time when things had been really bad for both of them, and he had been vulnerable to St. Augustina in a way she had never seen again since.

"She's out there. And she's safe," he said.

"You sound really sure about that?" she asked, going very still. The way he had said it ... did that mean he had found her?

He quirked an amused eyebrow. "What's the point of being a Saint if I don't have faith?"

St. Augustina snorted, encompassing her entire opinion on everything he had just said. Jackass was messing with her again.

She finished her plate of savory food, not a scrap left on it, and exchanged it for the pie. She knew she was exaggerating her nonchalance. She wanted nothing more than to storm out and put a city's worth of distance between

them, except it was always a bad idea to run from a predator. Besides, she wasn't going to let him run her off from her pie. This was her table, dammit; she would leave when she was damn well ready and not a nanosecond before. He could leave first.

Carefully, she cut through the chocolate fluff of her ill-gotten dessert with the side of her fork, giving the truly simple task her full, unwavering attention. At the same time, his food finally appeared. For a moment, while he pulled the toothpick holding his sandwich together, she wondered if that was really the end of the questions. Still, she realized that with a job like this, knowing as much as she already did, they weren't going to let her simply walk away.

For a moment, she thought about letting whoever "they" were come and try to silence her. She'd relish the fight. Just for a moment, though.

Going up against a powerful organization—which is what the Orange Lady had to represent to have that kind of money to throw around—was an entertaining thought, but other than her life, St. Augustina couldn't afford to waste her resources on something that wasn't going to pay. And St. Benedict knew that. She could curse herself for not getting up and walking out the moment she saw him or shooting him in his smug face.

"There is a carrot," he said, recapturing her attention. "We both know that it would cost you something to walk away, but there is also a golden carrot in this job for you."

"The money..."

"No," he interrupted, holding up his hand, then forming a pointed finger, "something better. Something lasting." He let his pause draw out, his smiling, green-blue eyes looking deep into her bronze ones.

She refused to ask the question, but his smile deepened. He could see it in her eyes. Slipping his Saint Box out from under his shirt, he held it up for her to look at, swinging gently from the end of his chain.

"A choice."

Her eyes darted to it. Her throat tightened. Her heartbeat doubled, and her mouth went dry.

He was offering her freedom.

"You have your Saint Box?" Carefully, she licked her lips, wishing she had a better poker face, but that was the problem with St. Benedict. When he offered something in a deal, it was always something he believed he could deliver.

"What is the job again? In better detail this time," St. Augustina asked.

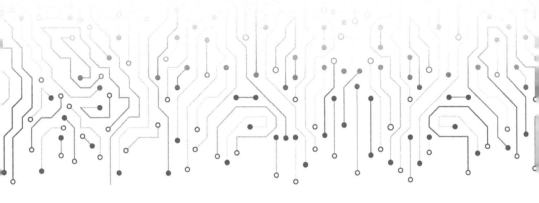

CHAPTER 2

There was a light drizzle as they left the diner. St. Augustina turned to look up at the grey night sky, letting the water kiss her face a moment, before sliding her hood up over her braided hair. The LEDs on her hood came to life on the edge of her perception. She slipped on her goggles, in case she needed to activate her augmentation, shielding her eyes from the light. One would think the goggles would destroy her peripheral vision, but they had the added advantage of projecting tiny displays showing what was beside and behind her simultaneously. Literal eyes on the back of her head and well worth the extra credits they had cost.

Feeling more confident, she turned to walk down the street, being at the top of a steep hill that curved back about a mile and a half into the crowded heart of Infinity Corners. There were dozens of shops and stalls still open, with plenty of customers milling in and out of the river of traffic. Whatever space was not occupied by merchant booths was filled with fast -moving, rotating adverts projecting themselves in light at the walking target markets, constantly scanning and modifying themselves to target the majority preferences.

St. Benedict fell in beside her, readjusting his fedora as he went. His eyes glowed blue again. "Do you need anything for the job?" he asked, nodding at an open bin of cheapy microchips laid out on display next to some knock-off gold watches.

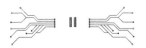

"No, I'm ready to go right now. The sooner we get done with this, the sooner I can watch my life expectancy go up," she said.

"Just having me here has already doubled it," he replied, so she slid her foot sideways along the ground and tripped him.

"Oh, sorry," she said blandly, as he stumbled and almost face-planted into a pair of courtesans, themselves out to rustle up some customers. They giggled and flirted all over him and his pretty face, while St. Augustina waited by a cinnamon nut stall. It was the height of hilarity to watch suave, smooth St. Benedict behave like an awkward teen, ducking away from one of the ladies who tried to lay a "teaser" kiss on him. They only gave up after he rejoined St. Augustina, taking her presence as the deterrent it wasn't.

"Still celibate, I see," she quipped as she popped a cinnamon nut in her mouth.

"Still," he agreed. "You?"

"Mostly yes, though not by my choice."

"The tragedy of a career-minded woman?" he asked, then pointed to the small packet in her hands. "Still hungry?"

"They smelled good. And I was really engrossed in the show," she said, indulging in another one and pointedly turning when he went to help himself to one.

Before he could quip back, they both froze: St. Augustina first, St. Benedict a second later. Dark forms had infiltrated the crowd, taking up positions where they would be the most innocuous, moving along and through without disturbing the surrounding people.

"Ninjas?" St. Benedict asked quietly.

"Neo-ninjas," St. Augustina corrected.

"If they were neo-ninjas, would we have sensed them at all? Their cloaking tech should have blinded our augmentations to their presence."

"Except, not to me," St. Augustina shared, "you only noticed them after I did."

"You mean a Saint Link? That's only theoretical," St. Benedict countered, following her lead as she turned and casually began to walk with the crowd again. Accordingly, the dark shadows followed, assured that they had not been spotted yet.

"And how are you able to see them?"

St. Augustina only smiled as she added, "None of your business. And I can't believe you are still arguing against the Saint Link."

"There is no concrete evidence that it is a thing. I don't believe in things I can't quantify," St. Benedict slid around behind St. Augustina, switching sides smoothly so that she would be free to draw her gun and turn when the time came. "It's just training and familiarity. Everything else is superstition and hearsay."

"Anecdotal evidence is still evidence," she countered as she turned in concert with him into and through a holographic advertisement between two storefronts, which had been hiding an alley full of garbage from the street.

"Eyewitness accounts are unreliable."

"As unreliable as you are?"

"Okay, are you going to harp at me the entire job?"

She gave a half-shrug as she picked her way through the garbage, stepping on only the most stable looking pieces. Wouldn't do to twist an ankle right before being ambushed. She could still sense the dark eyes watching them, feel their pressure as the neo-ninjas continued to position themselves to strike. Who sent them was irrelevant, but St. Augustina thought she had counted somewhere between five and seven on the ground, three to six watching from above.

Funnily enough, not a whole lot about this situation seemed real. She had fought neo-ninjas before and in back alleys no less, but having St. Benedict at her back really stretched her imagination.

There was a bend in the alley, and St. Augustina was not at all surprised when they rounded the corner to find six dark figures waiting silently in a vee shape. Legs apart with their arms akimbo, hands clasped behind their backs. It was an intimidating sight. They were garbed completely in dark, tight-fighting clothing, neutralizing any sign of their humanity. Even their eyes were obscured by two oily black orbs, compu-lenses that allowed them to see more than the average human could, both in the real world and in the cyber world. A shimmer passed over their forms. The tech-cloaking digital miracle worked into the fiber of their clothes masked everything from body heat to bodily excretions to the electromagnetism everyone generated; they were nothing more than deadly shadows waiting.

So why did St. Augustina sense them? Truth be told, she just did. She always had. Some strange miswiring, perhaps, in her augmentations that gave her a fortuitous edge. She had no interest in having someone poke around in her artificial parts to figure it out for her. Certainly, if anyone with interest in such things caught wind of the ability, she would be dissected on a cold slab as fast as money could exchange hands.

It was fun being different.

St. Benedict's back bumped into hers as he shifted his position.

"How many?" she asked softly.

"Three."

"Six up front. I doubt that's all of them."

"Who knows? We could get lucky, and they've underestimated us..."

St. Augustina outstretched her hand over her shoulder at him, igniting it with a yellow light. "Sync up with me," she ordered.

"Well, I suppose you *did* buy me dinner first," St. Benedict mock-sighed. "Guess I gotta put out now." He shifted a bit, and she imagined he was

yanking off his leather glove before passing his palm over hers, ignited with his own blue light. She blinked three times and felt the tiny tingle over her eyes as yellow light filled her vision for a brief moment, then a digital overlay covered the world. In a small corner of her sight appeared another view that showed the three other dark forms that St. Benedict saw through his eyes.

"My targeting system isn't picking them up," he complained as he squinted a bit, like that would actually make it work better.

"Attack where you don't see them," she said, replacing her hand back over the grip of her R-pistol. The safety was already off, but it reassured her to finger it again as they both waited for someone to act first.

The drizzle above turned into proper rain, soaking the alley and the garbage. Lightning and thunder crashed simultaneously.

St. Augustina moved before her thoughts had caught up that she had. With a dead run that only needed three steps to get up to speed, she leapt, bouncing off of the wall to come at them at an angle over the partial triangle of six. She pulled her pistol out of her coat in one smooth motion, firing a small burst of beam shots. She didn't expect to actually land any of her shots as she passed over the scattering targets. It was gratifying to see three shots actually hit.

What? Had the ninjas fallen asleep waiting for her to move?

They scattered into the garbage, temporarily disappearing from her sight, not just her targeting program. All except one, who had taken a bolt full in the shoulder, damaging the tender fabric of his suit and leaving enough of him exposed to feed her the smallest heat signature for her programs to track.

From the corner of her sight, she saw St. Benedict had engaged with his three as well. He had gone with more of a gunslinger approach. He knelt, whipped out two laser pistols, and fired alternating green and purple bursts. Not one of them hit. He dropped and rolled to his right. His three chose to rush him instead of scattering, which was a mistake on their part. He was pretty slippery up close.

Refocusing, St. Augustina barely had time to react as a neo-ninja dropped onto her from above, his sword bearing down. There was an electric crackle as she smoothly unsheathed her own energy knife while she turned. The neo-ninja's inertia sent her falling back into one of the piles of garbage. A bag of something truly disgusting burst underneath her weight, and St. Augustina gagged as the breath was knocked out of her. She brought her knee up, nailing the ninja firmly in the solar plexus. A strangled gasp came from her opponent, and the pressure of the ninja blade lessened, giving her the opportunity to avoid getting pinned by kicking out with her other leg.

The neo-ninja flew away, propelled by her inhuman strength, just in time for two others to bear down on her. She had already rolled through the mound of garbage and reappeared on the other side.

Regaining her feet, she pivoted and fired off another short volley. The war gods were with her as the one she had kicked away took several of the shots and fell backward, dead. The two chasing her disappeared into the mounds of garbage. She sent a few shots their way for good measure.

"Hey, a little help!" St. Benedict called out. There was a great deal of confused movement from his view cam, and she pivoted again to see him struggling a few feet further in the alley. His three opponents had multiplied into six, two of which had managed to pin his arms. They were still struggling to get in close and completely immobilize him. He was doing a good job, forcing the two holding him to bear his weight as he continued the fight with just his legs.

Extending the length of her energy knife to its full three feet, she rushed toward the combatants, her augmented legs boosting her speed. She fired off a few more shots before engaging them in hand-to-hand. Two of the neo-ninjas arched backward, spasming as the shots penetrated their suits.

She wasn't sure if St. Benedict saw her coming, but their synced timing could not have been more perfect. He shoved off one of his attackers with a double roundhouse kick that propelled the neo-ninja onto her incoming blade. There was no resistance as the blade passed through, stopping only when the hilt of the burning beam hit the body. The tip of the blade was an inch away from St. Benedict's exposed chest. The move placed her face-to-face with the last neo-ninja, who was still holding onto Saint Benedict's right arm.

"Yield and go. Now," she said, her voice deadly. The glow from her eyes shining out through the goggles tinged the edges of their enemy's black hood. There was only a heartbeat of time before the ninja dropped St. Benedict to the ground.

A piercing scream cut through the smelly air. St. Augustina dared to turn her head just a fraction, still cognizant of the threat before her. The awful sound degraded into something between metal grinding metal and a horse's whinny. At the far end of the alley stood a tall shadow. Squinting hard at the overly bright backdrop of light from the street, St. Augustina thought it looked like a unicorn, which was absurd. Smoke of some sort billowed around its stamping but soundless hooves. Something appeared to be wrong with its feet, but daring to turn her head even more, she had to double-take as her periphery caught the sight of the neo-ninjas disappearing into a cloud of ever-thickening smoke.

The apparition trumpeted again, but it too was gone by the time she turned fully toward it.

Panting, St. Augustina stood in the alley, her gun and her energy knife in either hand, every muscles tense as she waited for a renewed attack to come. It never did.

The bodies of the vanquished neo-ninjas had also disappeared into the night.

"Are they gone?" St. Benedict asked.

"Probably," she answered, lowering her weapons.

Truthfully, St. Augustina was fairly confident they were. To lose one of their number was a disgrace. Losing four meant they had entirely lost face. But to lose the entire unit in one fight was simply tactically stupid. So, they had retreated. Frankly, that was the least of her worries. The apparition, though...

"You saw that thing, right?" she asked, turning to St. Benedict, who was still lying on the ground. She knelt on one leg, retrieving one of her weapons, checking it mindlessly as he caught his breath. The whole of the fight had taken less than five minutes, but that was the nature of fights. They were an eternity in a heartbeat.

"Yes. Do you know what that was?" he asked, looking up at her face, studying her.

She shut down her knife and returned it to her utility belt. "Trick of tech, obviously."

"Tech?" St. Benedict sounded derisively flabbergasted.

"Well, it wasn't magic, so what else could it have been?"

"How do you know?"

"Because there is no such thing as magic, now get up," she snapped, rolling her eyes.

He double blinked at that statement, settling back onto his haunches instead of doing what she ordered. She almost quit right there in disgust. She had no time to deal with superstitious nonsense.

"If you say so," he finally said carefully, as if she were the crazy one. "Then what was it? We both saw it."

"Ocular interference, obviously. To make us think we saw something that isn't there. I'm sure it was their calling card, or maybe whoever hired them."

St. Benedict nodded, accepting her logic.

"Thank you, St. Augustina," St. Benedict added, breathing out a sigh of relief, as he pushed himself up to his feet. "I'm not kidding, they had me dead in their sights. I could barely keep up with them. Half the time, I wasn't even sure what I was seeing was real until they had my arms pinned."

Seizing his jaw, St. Augustina examined the cuts on his chin and eyebrow ridge with the medical assessor in her augmented vision.

"Looks like you'll live. We got lucky. They were badly trained. Relied too much on their suits to hide them than any actual skills," she said, slipping a finger into a small pouch against her thigh and pulling out a finger full of bio-plaster to coat over St. Benedict's cuts, sealing them until they healed. His own fingers followed up to capture hers to get her to look into his eyes, still glowing iris-less blue.

"Thank you. I mean it," he said, giving her a little squeeze.

She flinched away. "What the hell is wrong with you?"

She turned to flounce off, tracking a new path through the now-scattered garbage. She really needed a shower. The sooner they got out of the alley, the better she would feel. She needed to finish this job and get home to do some laundry or something.

Once they hit the street, it was back to casually weaving through the shopping traffic and vehicles trying to move through too little space. Ignoring the screwed-up nose of a vendor she passed, St. Augustina hoped it had more to do with her sudden appearance than any lingering odor. It might cost less to buy a new coat instead of fronting the cost to get her current one dry cleaned.

"So, do you get attacked by ninjas often, neo or otherwise?" St. Benedict asked, striking up a fresh casual note.

"Only when I take badly planned jobs," she muttered, giving him a sideways glance. He rubbed at the plaster just over his eye, smoothing out the edges until it blended completely into his face.

"Now imagine them coming after you, and you hadn't taken the job? I wouldn't have been with you," he said.

"I would have been fine."

"Oh, come on, I distracted three or six of them for you. I was very helpful."

"Who employed them?" she asked, more to herself, ignoring his joke.

Upon coming to a possible conclusion, she turned and shoved her unsuspecting companion, pinning him against the closest wall. A group of young men came out of the door just down the way from them at that same exact moment and began hooting and hollering.

"Woohoo! Go get him, girl!" they catcalled and laughed, making rude gestures as they disappeared into the crowd. St. Benedict's eyes twinkled, which just made it worse. She didn't let him go.

"Who are we up against, St. Benedict?"

He stared up at her too long, his eyebrows furrowed as if he was trying to figure out what to say. "I don't know." He put his hands up in surrender. "I honestly don't know."

She let him go and took a step back. The knowing smiles of passers-by were starting to get to her. He straightened his fedora in that nervous gesture he used to collect himself.

"Look, I could feed you a mysterious line about a shadowy counter team or machinations of a dark corporate conspiracy theory, and they would all be plausible. I know as much as you do. We need to go get the data package. It contains codes that could literally make or break the world we are both occupying right now, as we both know it."

"How do you know it's that important?" St. Augustina asked, her stomach sick with dread.

"How could it not be? They threw neo-ninjas at us," he countered.

"That's not an answer."

"It's the best one I have at the moment. You want more answers, I suggest we go fetch the data package and take a look at it ourselves. Maybe it'll be obvious once we get it."

He was lying. Somehow, someway, she knew he was lying, but she couldn't figure out about what, or what it could, would, should mean. "Fine. Fine. Where are we going?" she asked.

"There." He pointed up at a towering building, blinking with various neon lights against the grey cloudy sky. Written in blinking block letters of shaped neon were the words "OverClock."

CHAPTER 3

elcome to OverClock! Have you played with us before?"

"Yes."

"No."

The two Saints looked at each other, flashing exact mirrors of consternation at the other.

"Yes, we have," St. Benedict repeated, not looking away from his partner for a moment, before turning back to the Game Master with his signature award-winning smile, a combination of charming flirt and boy-next-door. One would think that a woman, dressed in what basically amounted to glowing green straps that covered exactly enough to barely pass for any corporate decency regulations, would be incapable of blushing, except St. Augustina watched the telltale pinkening sweep up and down the woman's whole body, not just her cheeks. The female Saint had to wonder, if they hadn't checked their garbage-coated coats at the check-in, would the Game Master have the same reaction?

"Do you have... have..." she stuttered, searching the standing desk in front of her for brains, or maybe a sense of self-awareness.

"An invitation?" St. Benedict offered, flipping up a clear, plastic ticket with neon print all over it and a barcode at the bottom. With a wink, he presented it to her like a playing card, pincered between his first two fingers. St. Augustina kicked him in the shin, but while his body shifted, he didn't break

eye contact or dim his smile. All it did was make the Game Master double blink. A calculation passed over her eyes, the only part of her not made up, before she took the invitation with a semblance of professionalism.

Inserting it into her desk, which also doubled as her machine, they all waited a moment for a response.

St. Augustina took the opportunity to look around, slipping her goggles up to rest against her hairline. The whole facility was motiffed in a retro-futuristic style with round-edged corners on everything. The images of the more popular OverClock avatars moved across the walls. It was a neat effect, one the OverClock company had patented, so St. Augustina had only seen it once or twice before. All the other Game Masters servicing other players were dressed much like their own Game Master, all in costumes made from materials that seemed like they were originally intended to be at a construction site, and someone had the brilliant idea to repurpose into clothing. One young man, with a handsome but rat-like smirk and blond hair, but not much else, guided two women down a neon-lined hall. Retro Grunge at its worst.

St. Augustina kind of liked it.

The desk binged and returned the invitation.

"All set," the Game Master chirped, handing the invitation back, before indicating a hallway behind her. "Your private room has already been paid for. When you are ready, take a left, then another left. It'll be the room with the devil icon on the door."

St. Benedict paused, then looked down at the invitation before muttering under his breath, "The Orange Lady has a sense of humor."

"Are we ready to go?" St. Augustina asked, and he nodded, gesturing the way with an open palm.

"You first, My Lady," he said, giving a gallant bow that was out of place with his techie clothes and noir hat.

As they moved down the hallway, excited cries and laughter echoed from some of the rooms. They passed a larger room with dozens of open jack-in chairs, a few with groups of people around them watching the screens in front of the chairs and cheering as things became exciting.

"You're grinning?" St. Benedict noted when St. Augustina paused to peek into the semi-darkened room.

"I haven't played a game in … a long time seems like an understatement." She touched the silver box around her neck, making it clink inside. "I used to play all kinds of console games when I was in high school. Was actually pretty good too."

"I'd believe that. Shooters?"

She gave a half-shrug. "Sometimes. I actually preferred platformers and puzzle games. You know, stuff that had a point. I'd do shooters if my friends were playing. That's the only time it was fun because we could all be on the same team."

"I'm glad to hear you say that," he said, laying a hand on her shoulder to encourage her to continue on down the hall.

"Do I dare ask why?"

"Of course you dare; you're the Saint of Badassery, right?" he grinned.

"And you're the Saint of Not-Answering-Direct-Questions."

"We're doing a private game today. Still on the public server, but definitely more puzzle than shoot-'em-up."

"Then why am I here?"

"For the shoot-'em-up parts, while I'm hacking the puzzles."

They came to a door with a big, glowing-red stencil of a devil's head, grinning and winking, right smack in the middle of it. A small, black key box sat right above the rounded handle, and into that, St. Benedict deposited the invitation. The door gave another pleasant little bing and opened itself, swinging inward.

"Welcome!" a warm voice chimed, and the darkened room came to life. It was an eight-by-eight square space with four jack-in chairs facing inward. Along the back wall was a shelf prepped with various drinks and snacks as well as a standing menu for meals and another for various drugs or alcohols. The chairs themselves were white on the outside and upholstered with soft black on the inside. They were shaped like loungers for extended use, and an armature protruded from each one, holding a private viewing screen that was currently blank. They all seemed to be in good condition, with only the smallest signs of wear on the edges.

Overall, it all looked very classy.

"Swank," St. Augustina said and drifted to the back wall to select a bottle of fancy bubble water. Before she cracked the top, she paused. "Are these refreshments included in the room or extra?"

"Included, no worries," St. Benedict said, shutting the door. Then he did something curious. He began to gesture at the door. Since he nearly always had his augmented eyes on, St. Augustina didn't register what he was doing at first. He was interacting with augmented reality. Blinking thrice, she initiated her own sight.

Instantly, she tuned in to what he was seeing. A layer of holographic projection placed itself over the door. It looked like a circuit box, with holes and dials connected by various colored wires. Using his lit fingers, St. Benedict drew a line from a port to a different hologram hovering over his hand, connecting himself to the door's internal security.

"Is that necessary?" she asked, marveling at his cheek.

"You want someone coming in while we're jacked in?"

"Isn't that why I'm here?" She took a swig from the bottle.

"It's OverClock's security I'm more worried about. You still have your offensive programs, right?"

She didn't dignify that with an answer.

He tapped twice on a little mouse icon's head in his personal hologram set up. It immediately jumped up, gave a little salute and scurried down the cord, wiggling and whipping its tail as it seemed to visually squeeze into the circuitry in the box.

"They'll notice the breach into their network," St. Augustina said dryly.

He glanced at her over his shoulder. "Don't say that."

"Why the hell not?"

"Because it's bad for my karma. When you say bad things are going to happen, they do. So, cut it out. We're only at the beginning of the mission."

"Ha, I'm not God. I don't have that much power in this world."

St. Benedict waved his hand away, dismissing his link to the network in the door. "It may be superstition, but please indulge me."

"You've changed," St. Augustina said, taking a seat in one of the loungers.

He furrowed his brows. "You and St. Rachel say the same thing," he griped, taking the chair directly across from her.

That piqued St. Augustina's interest. "How did you convince her to follow you after your little rebellion?" she asked, leaning forward to prop her chin on her open palm.

"I didn't have to convince her of anything," he said, pressing some buttons on the underside of the screen for his chair. A panel popped off. "We were both sold and bought just like you."

"That's bullsh..."

"This isn't about me, St. Augustina. It's about you, okay? Just drop it," he snapped through his smiling teeth before removing an object from one of his pockets, unfolding it in his hands.

"What are you doing?"

He tapped his temples. "I still have the ocular hook up. Brought my own adapter." She could see once he had unfolded it, a camera with its own little arm that he snapped into a slot at the top of the chair.

"You didn't get that replaced?" St. Augustina was surprised. Her own link into digital networks was a port at the side of her neck attached to her spine, which was far safer. As far as she knew, St. Benedict was the only one to have an ocular connector, its tendency to fry the brain of the user way too high to warrant the convenience.

"I can't replace it. That's the downside of being the prototype," he said. "They installed it with no intention of taking it out again. Believe me, I checked."

"Yeah, but couldn't you just shut it down and have a secondary port installed instead?"

"Why are you so concerned about me?" he asked suggestively, the playful smile returning.

"I don't know. I guess I'm a forgiving soul," she replied, meeting his gaze with the cool indifference often seen in cats.

He nodded at that, keeping his thoughts to himself about it. "I'm ready."

Realizing she wasn't, St. Augustina swept up the loose cord beside her and snapped it into her port with a satisfying click. As much as she disliked what she had become, she still experienced a thrill when she logged her consciousness into a network.

Closing her real eyes, she relaxed and waited for the whoosh feeling that always danced down her body.

"You have to hit the green flashing button," St. Benedict called.

Jumping a little, she popped her eyes open again and slapped at the plastic-covered button that was indeed flashing green with the words "Let's go!" printed on it.

She barely got her eyes closed again before the whoosh feeling overtook her, like the surf of an ocean, pulling at her with its mighty tide through cool, delicious water. Breathing wasn't necessary. Her body would do that automatically. Soon enough, the world shifted again, and she found herself standing on a balcony above a huge pit. Blinking twice, she looked around. There were crowds of people and creatures all around, other players' avatars. They ranged from every sort of human to every kind of animal, non-human, or stylized object imaginable. Those that did not have custom avatars had done a lot of modification to templates. Two lion-like creatures strolled by on their hind legs, looking and moving exactly the same, except that one was bright green with a yellow mane, and the other was blood red and covered with tattoos and an eyepatch.

In the pit below was a battleground of some sort. It was set up like a mini jungle, complete with trees and vines and platforms at various, illogical heights. A vehicle or two was jammed into the undergrowth and all kinds of boxes and supplies were strewn about in what seemed like chaos, but was in fact all about chest height, forming walls to hide behind. Using such bulwarks were players, all different kinds of cartoonish characters, armed to the teeth with guns, knives, bombs and one clown seemed to be throwing deadly pies that smoked and hissed the minute they touched something.

"I thought we weren't going to play any war games?" St. Augustina asked the hero-type avatar standing next to her, his super square jaw, permanently gleaming smile, and twirly pompadour almost too ridiculous to look at directly.

"We're not," St. Benedict said from inside his avatar. He cast an eye on St. Augustina, looking up and down. "OverClock has an arcade of mini-games. That's where we're going today. You know, you're still in template mode."

She glanced down at her avatar's body. The program had defaulted to her actual appearance, a woman with warm, brown skin and its version of braids that were a lot more chunky and stylized than her actual hair. Otherwise, she wasn't surprised to see herself standing there in a thong and dark bra.

She sighed. "Chauvinism certainly is alive and well if this is the default."

"Here," St. Benedict said, stepping forward to swipe a menu up in front of her. After navigating a few pages with his fingers, he selected something, and her appearance instantly shifted. She was still herself, but she was dressed in a nut-brown woman's suit with a white blouse underneath and black boots peeking out from under slightly bell-bottomed pant legs. Her braids had also disappeared to be replaced with a full 'fro that haloed her head and hoopy earrings swung from her ears. "What do you think?"

"Full Foxy Brown?" she asked, pulling up a mirror program so she could see herself. A holographic version mirrored her, and she turned to look. "Feels like Halloween."

"We're not going to be here long, but if you want something else..."

"It's fine," she replied, feeling kind of badass as she dismissed the mirror program. "Like you said, we're not going to be here long."

"Okay, this way," St. Benedict said, heading down an infinitely curving hallway. He stopped and turned to pass through an archway made out of letters she wasn't able to read before they were in.

"Set your conversation mode to team-only," St. Benedict said.

"I did the minute we logged in."

"Oh. Good."

"And I have a question for you. I thought the job was for Core Processing," she said, as they walked past several game portals made to look like old-fashioned game cabinets. It was hard to tear her eyes from their colorful fronts, especially when so many of them were her favorite games.

"It is."

"This isn't where Core Processing is."

"Of course it is. There is very little Core Processing doesn't control anymore. It's all connected. We're here to pick up the package already prepared for us from another job. This isn't the really dangerous part yet," he said.

"And what happened to that other team that they needed to hide the package instead of removing it themselves?" she asked, crossing her arms.

St. Benedict paused, giving her a sideways look that told it all. "Best not to think about it," he said, before stopping in front of the cabinet for a game called "Operation Grandma."

"And they hid it in a game?" She nodded to herself. "I suppose that's clever."

"Very hard to detect if you don't know what you're looking for in the coding," St. Benedict agreed and tapped the *Player 2* button. "Come on."

St. Augustina shrugged and slapped the *Player 1* button. The world around them shifted, and she found herself in her grandmother's kitchen.

Not just any grandmother's kitchen. It was *her* grandmother's kitchen down to the smallest detail. From the yellow and white tile on the floor to the teal-colored fridge from the seventies that her grandfather had patched and rebuilt to keep it going. There was a smell of cookies, sugar, and cinnamon in the air. The old radio on a shelf in the corner was tuned to the really old oldies of some big band that St. Augustina did and did not recognize. The window was open, and a light summer breeze blew in gently, the shadow of leaves dancing across the sill.

"What the hell?!" St. Augustina declared, stepping back into the kitchen door that went to the garage. Nearly panicked, she tugged and twisted the knob, but it wouldn't budge.

"St. Augustina? Are you there?" The crackled voice of St. Benedict came from nowhere.

"What the hell?!" she demanded again.

"Something went wrong. I think it's my ocular connection. I'm going to jack out and jump back in," he said, or at least that was what she thought he said, his voice was breaking up so badly. Then it was gone altogether.

Standing in her grandmother's kitchen, St. Augustina struggled to take a full breath. Why was she panicking like this? Obviously... obviously, this was part of the simulation...

"Idrina? Is that you, dear?" her grandmother's voice called from the living room. St. Augustina stared at the white, paint-chipped door between the kitchen and the living room, her heart racing afresh. "Idrina?"

Woodenly, she moved to it. Grasping the handle, she attempted to turn it but found at the last second there was a lock on the door. Which was wrong. There shouldn't have been a lock of any kind on this door. It was a modern combination lock, not one that her grandmother would have ever used considering how bad her memory was. It was rectangular with the u-shaped bar looping out of the top. Along its right side were three dials, but instead of numbers, they were of letters.

The Saint stared at the lock and took three deep breaths. "It's a game," she whispered. "They're pulling all of this from my mind. It's just a game. Operation Grandma. It was right on the door." Looking around the kitchen, this time she could see the differences. There were letter magnets on the fridge that had never been in her grandmother's house. A cat that her grandmother never owned, because she hated cats, sat on the windowsill, lazily twitching its tail back and forth in a predictable pattern. It even had a name tag on its collar that read "Schrödinger." Her grandmother wouldn't have been that clever. And on a lower shelf from the radio was a metal cookie jar with various locks bolted in and all around it, holding the lid on.

Fetching the cookie jar off the shelf, she found a laminated card underneath. Printed on it was $3 = T$. She took both to the kitchen table. She hadn't expected to do puzzles on this job, but since she was here, it was something to do while St. Benedict worked on getting back into the simulation. Her job was supposed to be protecting him, but now she wished she had insisted that he give her the rest of the job details in full. When had she gotten so sloppy? Even if she had wanted nothing to do with this job in the first place, she had always been anal about knowing every detail before going in. And here she was making the same mistake again, with the same partner.

That's when she noticed the clock on the wall. Or rather the circle with an hourglass embedded in it, sand pouring from the top to the bottom.

Her grandmother definitely did not have one of those.

"Okay, so there is a deadline." St. Augustina proceeded to search the rest of the kitchen. Most of the shelves didn't open, but inside where she expected to find the silverware, she instead found an envelope with several playing cards.

"Idrina? Is that you?" her grandmother called again from the other room.

"Yes, grandma, it's me," she called back, feeling a little nauseous.

"Well, come in and say 'hi,' child."

"Be there in a minute."

Sitting at the table, she messed around with the playing cards for a moment until she realized that one of the locks on the cookie jar had four playing cards symbols on it. Arranging them in numerical order provided the right sequence, and she popped off the lock. Smiling toothily, she felt kind of proud of herself. Solving puzzles had been something she had loved once. It was what made the job she had to do fun for her. Sometimes.

"Idrina? Is that you?" her grandmother called again, in the same tone of voice and cadence as before. She wondered for a moment, if St. Benedict had managed to properly log in yet, whether it would be his grandmother in there or maybe an amalgamation of both, or would the program have still projected hers to her and his to his?

As it was irrelevant, she concluded, she needed to get on with solving the scenario. She needed to find more clues.

That was when she looked at the playing cards again and noticed something on the Ace of Hearts. At the bottom right-hand corner, someone had taken a red pen and written $2 =$ in front of the A. Picking up the other laminated card, she held it next to the playing card. $3 = T$. That drew her gaze to the cat on the windowsill, still purring and twitching its tail.

"I bet it's 'cat,'" she said, getting up from the table to turn the letters on the dial lock of the living room door. It clicked open with another satisfying snap. Maybe she didn't need St. Benedict after all. But where was this threat he was so certain he needed her for?

She set her hand on the doorknob, her heart clenched with apprehension. Stiffening her spine, she tightened her grip on the smooth, cool handle and turned, shoving the door open.

CHAPTER 3

Lights clicked on in her grandmother's living room, but no one was there. Blinking once, St. Augustina looked back into the kitchen and picked up the cookie jar before stepping to check behind the door. The room was empty of other people. Proceeding into the room, she looked over all the familiar knickknacks and the flowery furniture that never looked anything but old lady-ish. And the pictures. There were pictures everywhere, images of smiling kids and laughing adults. Picnics and fun at the beach. Graduations for St. Augustina and her brother and her step-sister, plus her five cousins. She wanted to linger longingly at all of them, but the image that she gravitated to the most was always the first one she saw whenever she was at her grandmother's.

In two silver and wood frames, on a little table by the beat-up, old piano, were the images of St. Augustina's mother. In one, she was dressed in an army dress uniform, looking noble, her chin uplifted, proud. Though she wasn't smiling, there was fire in her eyes. In the other picture, she was in her army fatigues and flight gear, holding her helmet and smiling broadly in front of her military helicopter. Set at a counterpoint to the two photos was her mother's bronze star, gleaming dully in the light.

How many hours had St. Augustina stared at these things while she waited at her grandmother's house for her father to come pick her up after he finished work, wondering where her mother was as she fought in a war no one really understood. Her parents had divorced shortly after her brother was born. She had been a little girl, so her mother and grandmother had been the more stable parts of her life. She couldn't have been prouder of her brave, warrior mother, who went into battle to rescue those lost in the fight. Honor, duty, bravery, and integrity were the four words that St. Augustina wanted to live her life by, such as it was, even if no one else understood who she was or what she was doing. And yet, having become a Saint, and doing the things that survival had required, St. Augustina daily felt like she failed to honor her mother. Honorable people don't take prisoners and torture them, or serve those who did. What did it say to her integrity that she had chosen to survive at the cost of any true sense of honor? What would her mother say?

Tears began to leak down her face upon seeing her mother's picture. Setting the cookie jar on top of the piano, she tried to brush them away, but all that accomplished was to scratch her face. It did nothing to stem the tide.

She dropped onto her grandmother's couch, continuing to weep in a way she hadn't in a long, long time.

She wished with every fiber of her being that she could talk to her mother. Truthfully, there had been an opportunity. If she really wanted it, she could make it happen, even take precautions so that no one from her world would find out. Why hadn't she?

Yet, she would never be able to explain all of what happened to her since she disappeared. So many times, she had wanted to walk out the door and let her feet take her home, but she knew that the moment she did, she would be walking off with an irreplaceable investment that the corporate overlords would never consent to let go entirely. Her mother would want her to come home, and she would have to say no.

Reaching up to clutch at her Saint Box, she started when she realized it was gone. But St. Augustina knew that. Why did she think she had been wearing it? She knew who had it and that she would never be able to get it back. She'd give anything to have it back.

Realizing that truth jarred others loose.

St. Augustina turned to look around the room, the one she knew was fake, but so exact down to the smallest detail.

"Where am I?" she asked out loud, at first to herself, then she repeated the question with the expectation that someone would answer her. "Hey! Where am I? What's going on?"

"Idrina?" a voice called, her grandmother's voice, but this time it came from the kitchen.

With urgency, she crossed the room, but almost the moment she moved, the door slammed itself shut. Black smoke puffed out of it when it closed, the crash echoing eerily as if it were in a larger space than the small living room. More smoke, thick and oily, began to permeate the room from the corners and from behind the furniture, family photos, and the various kitschy decorations. The acrid smell stung the back of St. Augustina's throat. She chewed on the inside of her cheek, desperate to make her mouth water so she wouldn't start coughing. Intuitively, she knew if she started, she would not stop.

Continuing to the door to the kitchen, she pulled hard on the knob, but like before, it was fixed into place as if it had never been made to twist or open.

"Idrina? Is that you?" her grandmother called again, her voice sounding like it was coming from the other side of the door, the same casual cadence as before.

"Grandma!" she shouted, which did make her start to cough.

The smoke devoured the walls. It boiled around the couch and end table in the middle of the room, both bobbling as if floating on a stormy ocean before they began to sink, swallowed whole by the too thick smoke. The light disappeared as the lamps were also taken, along with the shelves. Too late, St. Augustina thought of her mother's picture and shoved off the door, her arm uselessly stretched out to grab it. To her horror, she watched as the inky blackness took the small table. The picture floated defiantly above it for two or three seconds, and then her mother was gone, lost just inches beneath St. Augustina's reaching fingers.

"No!" she screeched impotently, gasping a sob she didn't realize was in that lump in her throat, as if it was actually her mother being swallowed. The darkness seemed to blurp up mockingly, to snap at her fingers. It was cold

and tingled like acid as it lightly dashed on her skin, before her enhanced reflexes could snap her hand away. The darkness gurgled as if it chuckled at her as it descended back into the mist-covered ground.

The smoke hovered at about hip height with tendrils of it floating up to obscure everything around her. This wasn't any sort of digital world anymore; the OverClock interface was completely gone. Checking her own body, she realized she was still wearing a pantsuit, but the stylized, cartoonish one was gone. Instead, she was dressed in her work uniform, a more modern woman's suit with polished, flat shoes and a silk blouse. It was what she had worn as an officer of the FBI, the one she last wore while she was on loan to the Kodiak Corporation. Even though her contract was technically held by the FBI, it was not uncommon for corporations with representatives on the City Council or other government positions to request the use of an agent or ten. It was not uncommon to borrow her and the team she led.

Her team.

Thinking she was about to vomit, she bit down on her tongue, letting the pressure focus her.

She remembered where she was. Her last assignment.

The Talent.

Rune Leveau.

Her task had been to seize the Talent.

Who reportedly knew the whereabouts of Anna Masterson.

The last remaining link to the Masterson Files.

What were the Masterson Files?

She didn't know. She never knew. It wasn't required to know.

The corporation wanted it. Badly.

She had done her job. Taken her team and pursued the Talent. Only, St. Benedict had gotten to the Talent first, and together, they had eluded capture.

So, St. Augustina, instead, arrested *his* team. It had been a smart move, and the leverage she needed to get the magic user…

Shaking her head, she remembered a simple truth about the *real* world she lived in.

Magic *was* real.

That was where she was, in a place of magic. Something called the Faerie Court. Attempting to escape some evil that had broken free, St. Benedict and his new Talent ally, Rune, had pursued her and her hostages into this place of darkness and evil magic. One by one, her team had died, devoured by the monster in the darkness.

Terror ripped through her. She pressed her fists against her temples and felt the rattle click in her skull as she realized her empty hand actually held a gun. An empty gun. She had fired every bullet she had, trying to protect her last man…

From "it."

"Johnson! Johnson! Where are you?" she shouted. Curse him! Curse St. Benedict for leaving her to die here.

Her only answer was the encroaching mist and shadows.

"Where are you!?" she roared.

The screeching whinny cut through the dense silence.

"You want me, then? Come and get me! I'm tired of waiting," she said, squaring her shoulders. She'd die kicking and screaming like the hell bitch she was.

"St. Augustina!" an echo screamed in the mist.

"St. Benedict?" As much as she loathed the man, the devil himself would be a welcome sight at the moment.

"The cookie jar! Grab the cookie jar!" she thought she heard, but his voice was degraded static, then completely gone.

"What?" But her eyes spotted it, a silvery spot in the mist, only a few feet from her. She dashed for it. The metal was burning cold, and she almost dropped it. Another scream in the mist, just in front of her and too close, forced her back, terror pounding through her chest.

Emerging from the darkness, its blood-red eyes glowed ethereally through the wisps of smoky mist. The unicorn-beast, the same one from the alley, stepped to the fore. Except it wasn't simply a unicorn, as if that was a simple thing in of itself. Instead of hooves, the creature had paws, like a lion, with great black talons crusted reddish with blood. Ichor dripped from its fanged mouth, falling to what felt to St. Augustina like turf beneath her shoes.

On instinct, she pointed her useless gun at the creature, tucking the cookie jar into the crook of her shoulder, like a precious baby she was determined to protect. The beast halted, not because it seemed to fear her threat, but because it had simply intended to stop. It regarded her silently. Snorting from its equine nose, whirls in the smoke spun out in elegant rolls. That's when St. Augustina realized the monster was snorting the mist itself, creating more.

"Well!? Well!?" she shouted in challenge. What the hell was it waiting for?

"Idrina?"

Spinning in place, St. Augustina had to check herself. She had almost shouted for her grandmother to run. Her grandmother, who wasn't there. But the door was.

Mist curled around it, much like a drunken seducer taking liberties on a lost virgin looking for their church group. There had been other doors in the mist. It had been part of the horror of the Faerie Court, doors standing alone, not connected to any walls, mocking symbols of escape that never opened as one by one, her team was murdered around her.

Yet, with no other options, she found herself stumbling toward it.

"You are mine," the unicorn-monster's voice rumbled through the mist. Or maybe it was the mist. Or maybe she had truly gone mad and only thought it spoke to her.

"No," she cried as she gripped the handle of the door, desperate for it to yield an inch.

"You will dream for me."

"No!" she screamed, banging hard on the door, with the butt of the gun. The smoke curled around her legs, its acidic cold seeping through her clothes, seeking out the scrapes in her skin to sink into. Losing control of her body, she turned toward the monster, now standing directly above her. Its blood-red eyes gleamed liquidly as it gazed down imperiously at her. Its breath was sickening, full of rot and decay. There was nothing she could do against it.

"Forget..." it intoned again. "You are mine. Forget."

The door behind her opened a crack. A crack and no further. It was too late, she couldn't move anymore. Couldn't fight.

"Not again, please," she begged uselessly as the cold penetrated her bones and then deeper to the place beyond her body.

"You are mine. Now, dream."

No, that wasn't right. There was one thing she could do.

"Dream. Dream."

She jammed the cookie jar through the crack, a move of pure illogic, but with certainty that it was the right one.

"You are mine."

CHAPTER 4

itting at the diner table, St. Augustina stared out the window at the city beyond. Night had fallen hours ago, but for her, it had been years since she had seen the real sun. In the distance, the movement of lights and neon created a serene picture, much like the waves of an ocean did for other people. The city shifted with its own rhythm.

The diner itself was perched on the edge of the Data Bowl, the quaint name some silicon genius had thought was clever to call it an age ago. The citizens of the city didn't seem to mind the name, humming along in their little lives amidst the wash of advertisements and the over-saturation of corporate propaganda.

Quiet moments like this weren't what St. Augustina lived for, any more. Settling back in the vinyl seat, she waited for her client. The auto-waitress had been by twice with the pot of synth-coffee. Though the thing was pre-programmed, she swore it was getting huffy that she hadn't ordered anything more.

If her client didn't show up soon, she was going to have to leave.

Except, she knew she wouldn't. It seemed like she had always been sitting at this booth, the seat especially grooved now for her derrière. Maybe she should just shell out the credits for a bowl of soup. She didn't need to take a shower today. Who was she trying to impress?

Fingering the chain of her Saint Box, she waited to hail the auto-waitress, when the door to the diner chimed open. A glowing woman entered, though that wasn't unique. Everything and everyone in the room had a glow to them. Even St. Augustina's coat had a lining of LED that would glow a gentle blue when she put it on, powered by kinetic movement or something. She wasn't really sure how it worked.

This woman glowed from head to toe with lights looped around her snug bodysuit and boots. Even in her hair, amongst her coiling dreads, were thick strings of orange lights. Turning her gaze to St. Augustina, even her eyes glowed orange with some sort of overlay contact. A teeny-bopper if ever she saw one.

This must be the client.

Nonchalantly, St. Augustina plucked up three tiny containers of hazelnut creamer, turning all her focus to peeling off the tiny lids and not on the woman as she approached the side of the table.

"St. Augustina?" the teeny-bopper asked.

"Depends on who is asking," she replied, then winced internally as she realized that she had just uttered the most cliché line in any spaghetti western ever.

Her potential client didn't seem to notice, as she cocked out one hip, setting some sort of container she was carrying on it. "I am the Orange Lady," she declared as if that should mean something to the Saint.

It did. It meant she was the person St. Augustina was waiting for.

"Have a seat," St. Augustina invited, dumping all three opened creamers into her black synth-coffee, watching it swirl in the darkness like white mist that brought in the light instead of darkness. Once the liquid was the same shade as the palms of her hands, St. Augustina gave it a sip, looking over the brim as the teeny-bopper plopped down hard, bouncing on the springs in the seat.

She set down a metal cookie jar with a too-loud *thunk* at the same time as she sat, which made St. Augustina pause mid-sip.

The jar was a queer thing. It had a shiny metal body with a two-inch-thick lid. Someone had pressed the metal with whimsical shapes of teddy bears and seals with balls on their noses at regular intervals around the body. Many shapes were marred, though, as someone had screwed in seven latches at regular intervals around it. All but one latch had a lock, and no two locks were the same.

"Okay, that's new," St. Augustina acknowledged, setting down her cup. She shifted her goggles over as if the cookie jar needed more space.

"Do you know what this is?" the Orange Lady asked, folding her hands on the table.

"Looks familiar," St. Augustina commented, and the Orange Lady's electric-orange lined eyebrows shot up. "I think my grandmother had one just like it."

The Orange Lady studied her a bit longer, and St. Augustina schooled her face to placid indifference. It was a bit unnerving to see the cookie jar, even more so to see it marred like that.

"You think this is your grandmother's cookie jar?" the Orange Lady asked.

Of course, it *wasn't* actually her grandmother's cookie jar. "Whoever made them probably made thousands of them. That's how manufacturing works," St. Augustina said dryly.

Right on cue, the auto-waitress zipped up to the table, its little waitress hat a bit off-centered on its silvery domed self.

"CAN I GET YOU ANYTHING?" it said, still sounding impossibly annoyed.

"Yes," the newcomer said, and ignited her hand with orange light that she passed over the thing's "head."

"UNLIMITED ACCESS," it intoned.

Gently, the Orange Lady straightened the auto-waitress's stylized hat. "I'll have an ice cream sundae, lots of chocolate sauce, and no cherries."

"ICE CREAM. CHOCOLATE SAUCE. NO CHERRIES. ANYTHING ELSE?"

"What would you like?" the potential client asked, making an inviting gesture to St. Augustina.

She double-blinked, then gave a tiny shrug. "Ten-ounce steak with a loaded baked potato."

"PLANT PROTEIN STEAK, ACCEPTABLE?"

"I didn't expect you to have anything different."

"THANK YOU FOR YOUR ORDER," the auto-waitress said, then zipped off.

"Thank you for dinner," St. Augustina added. "That's very kind of you." Unlimited access was no joke. Whomever this Orange Lady was, she had more than credits. Unlimited access meant she could take what she wanted from whatever machine she wanted. The keys to the kingdom. Only a few of the upper, upper elites had such a thing, and it was carefully monitored and regulated. Which made the Saint wonder, if this potential client wanted something under-the-table or nefarious done, why was she creating a record of her meeting with someone designed for exactly that purpose.

So, she was either naïve, or this was a trap.

Then there was that cookie jar.

As if she felt the Saint's eyes on it, the teeny-bopper rested a hand on the lid.

"Do you know what this is?"

"You already asked that."

"Yes, but answer me again anyway," she asked, batting her eerie orange eyes.

Sighing, St. Augustina regarded the metal jar, looking at it closer. "It's a metal container, presumably once intended to be a cookie jar, that someone has screwed on seven latches with various locks. One of which has already been undone." She paused a breath, considering. "It seems like one of those things found in an escape room or something."

"Very interesting that you would say that," the Orange Lady said. Her fingers rested primly on the edge of the table, like little cat paws. Each finger was lacquered with bright, glowing orange paint. It was even cuter when she rested her chin on top of her fingers, looking up at St. Augustina child-like.

The Saint resisted the urge to shift uncomfortably. She wasn't sure what kind of game this Orange Lady was playing, but it was too common in this city for something or someone so cute to turn out to be extremely deadly.

"Does this have anything to do with the job you were offering?"

Her potential client bolted upright, grinning from ear to ear. "Yes, indeed. This," she said, laying her hands around the fat belly of the cookie jar, "was obtained on a previous retrieval, but we can't open it."

"Take it to a locksmith. Or better yet, just get yourself a set of bolt cutters," St. Augustina said dryly. This was starting to feel like a joke.

"Won't work," the Orange Lady chirped.

"Why not?"

"Because it's augmented reality."

That pulled St. Augustina up short. Okay, that was a new one.

"Excuse me?"

"This." The Orange Lady gestured a big circle all around the cookie jar like it had its own private force field. "It's not actually here. It exists in augmented reality."

St. Augustina furrowed her eyebrows, then stuck out a finger and gently poked at the canister. It wobbled up and came back down with a tiny *thunk* on the table.

"Seems real enough to me."

"Its program is designed to send signals to your implants, tricking your brain into believing that what you see and feel is really there."

Goosebumps skittered up St. Augustina's skin as she stared at the cookie jar, the implication giving it a sinister aspect now.

The auto-waitress returned, bearing two plates that it set down correctly in front of them and an ice cream sundae from a third arm that disappeared into its backside as soon as it unloaded its burden. St. Augustina blinked for a moment, her eyes widening as she swore she saw the Orange Lady's plate slip through the cookie jar. The whole jar seemed to blink, then slid itself sideways as if the plate had shifted it.

"WILL THERE BE ANYTHING ELSE?" the auto-waitress asked. St. Augustina ignored it. Picking up her fork, she poked at the cookie jar with the tines, right into a smiling teddy bear face. It passed right through. Dropping the fork with a clatter, she immediately tried to force her hand through, and it stopped against cool metal, resisting against her skin as she pushed it closer to the edge of the table. If she kept pushing, would it fall off? Her fascination neared manic terror as the jar approached the edge. Then the teeny-bopper's hand stopped the progression toward doom, gently countering her small amount of strength on the other side.

"Amazing, isn't it?" she said with a gentle smile. "I've never seen anything like it."

St. Augustina sat back, returning her hand to her lap, reeling her existential crisis back in slowly like the stretched line of a fishing rod. Somehow, the Orange Lady wiggling with youthful delight seemed to help.

"Actually, I'm finding all of this fascinating," she chirped. "I've never seen a place like this before." Her hand washed the air, indicating the diner.

"I suppose you are used to the finer things in life," St. Augustina said, grasping for some semblance of normalcy and settling for something negative.

The Orange Lady didn't take offense. "You seem a bit shook up," she laughed.

"It's just..." Like magnets, St. Augustina's eyes went to the cookie jar. "It's nothing. New technology can be..." She cleared her throat. "It's nothing. I had the same reaction to my implants." Probably too much information, but she felt compelled to give more of an explanation. She cleared her throat again. "This is very cutting-edge tech. To make a person feel what's not really there."

"Yeah, I know, right!"

"Where did you get it?" St. Augustina's tone sharpened, startling the Orange Lady. The tactic seemed to work. Her potential client stuttered the truth before schooling herself.

"I... well... the other team..."

"What happened?"

The Orange Lady straightened, finally taking this more seriously.

"We lost someone on the original team. The other member is trapped. They managed to get this out to us before they were both taken."

Okay, that statement needed unpacking.

"Several questions." St. Augustina let that statement hang there as she cut herself a bite of the Protein Steak. It smelled heavenly. She wished she could give it the attention it deserved.

"I suppose I'll start with the most important. What is that thing supposed to be then? You say it's AR, but that's just its packaging isn't it?"

"Indeed, this jar contains information I need, wrapped up in this security program. We need to breach it."

"Made to look like one big metaphor," St. Augustina said around her bite. It tasted heavenly too.

"I suppose so." The Orange Lady ran her finger along the locks, making them click against the side. "All of these need to be undone to open it. They are security programs, or like... firewalls... apparently."

"I'm not much of a hacker. I can maybe find you some referrals."

"That's alright, I already know who I need to get, that's why I need you. This was supposed to be a three-part job. The first part of the job is done, but two more remain."

"If you already know the person you need, why are you talking to me and buying me steak?" St. Augustina furrowed her eyebrows, not liking where this was going. In fact, the hairs were rising up in her arms, and she had no idea why.

"The person we need is the other team member that was captured."

"You mean, the one you didn't get killed."

The Orange Lady nodded. "Yes, he has the keys to the locks. I need you to retrieve him for me."

"And does 'he' have a name?"

"I'd ... rather not give it to you."

"Then, I'd rather not do the job."

"My understanding is he is someone you are more inclined to shoot on sight than to rescue, and we desperately need him alive."

"I see." St. Augustina fetched the bottle of ketchup from its little stand on the table, buying herself some thinking time. She was about to ruin a good steak for it. "I suppose that depends then, on how good the incentive is for me to not shoot him. I have a shortlist of kill-on-sight people, but I can't think of anyone without a buy-off price."

"What do you want?"

"Freedom," St. Augustina answered, surprising herself. Where did that come from?

The Orange Lady cocked her head to the side curiously. "And what does freedom look like to you?" she asked.

"Never mind. I don't know what I said by that..." Then she stopped, catching her misspeak.

"What you *said* by that," the Orange Lady mused, humor thick in her voice.

"Meant by it..." Dammit if St. Augustina's ears weren't burning.

"You're a cute kid," the Orange Lady chirped. "Well, whatever you said or meant by that, I swear to fulfill it."

"What does that mean?" How had this conversation gotten so weird and disjointed?

"Whatever you say it means. When the time comes, you only have to name it, and it's yours. Do we have a deal? You rescue our friend, and I will ensure your freedom." The Orange Lady held out her hand, her orange nails glowing in the surreal light of the bar.

St. Augustina received the fingers with a small, curt squeeze. "I suppose we do."

"Great! I will pass you this then." The teeny-bopper slid the cookie jar toward St. Augustina. "I'll leave it to you to rescue St. Benedict and deliver it to him."

"St. Benedict?!" Suddenly, St. Augustina really regretted the deal. She thought she'd at least finish her meal before that happened.

"Yes," the Orange Lady nodded, standing up, her sundae untouched. Then she offered her hand to shake again. "I'll be in touch."

St. Augustina tried to take the hand to shake it, but instead, it ignited orange with light, and a data transfer passed between them.

"I don't know his whereabouts for sure, but this information should help you. I'll see you soon." Then the Orange Lady turned and flounced out with no further preamble.

Unsettled, the Saint had little else she could do but attempt to finish her meal. It sounded like she was going to need the calories for this job. Luckily, the ice cream sundae was in a perpetual self-refrigerating glass and would wait for her to finish the main course.

CHAPTER 5

While she finished eating, St. Augustina ignited her augmentation over her eyes. She usually preferred to make it as big as an actual desk, to give herself as much room as possible to work. Inside a diner, where she was doing something of questionable legality, she kept the holodesk down to the minimal setting. That created a circular display around her head and about a foot in front of her eyes, leaving her hands free to continue eating.

Reading the briefing the Orange Lady had passed her in the data transfer, she poignantly ignored the cookie jar for now. The brief floated in front of her, an eight by ten piece of paper made of light, with an opaque back to ensure only those facing it could read the information there. Her encryption software prevented anyone from casually picking up the data from it with a cloner.

She was relieved that her new employer had deemed it relevant to give her the details of the first run. Too many times, the perceived need for secrecy got in the way of getting the pertinent information that made the job more survivable.

The brief itself was quite a "page-turning thriller." It was, in fact, a long paragraph about the first job. St. Benedict and one other agent, the one that was eliminated, had gone into OverClock's main facility to hack Core Processing, the parent company, and retrieve a data package.

The second agent's name had been redacted, which was strange, and the light tinkering she did with the redaction add-on only got her three letters, so she wasn't able to even take a guess on who it was. She just hoped it wasn't someone she knew; that would have sucked. Instead, she focused on the description of the current job. The intent had been to retrieve the data package, which had been hidden inside a video game simulation. St. Benedict and the agent had entered the game, but St. Benedict had been detected almost immediately by the OverClock system and neutralized. What happened to the second agent was unclear. All that was known was that she went inside the simulation, and only the data package had come out. Obviously, it had been retrieved, though the briefing didn't specify by whom.

Furrowing her eyebrows, St. Augustina ate the last of her potato and snapped her fingers. A holo-keyboard appeared under her fingertips, and she began typing away.

Where was the body? If the second agent had gone into a VR simulation and the consciousness had not come out, there would have been the empty shell of a body still left abandoned somewhere in the facility. A quick search of the city network news showed that there was no mention of a dead body at the OverClock facility.

A dead body wasn't necessarily newsworthy, but one found dead inside a computer simulation? OverClock must have shelled out some major credits to make that bit of news disappear, and on top of that, been really lucky, because, even with unlimited access, sensational deaths were incredibly hard to hide. Humans do love their fantastical stories, even more than wealth, sex, or drugs.

Still, time was the great equalizer, or so she had been told. All it would take would be an ambitious investigative reporter with a juicy tip to dig up the cover-up. Plus, she was curious. She only had her employer's word, after all. The brief had very little detail on the matter of the first agent, which meant little miss teeny-bopper was either assuming a termination or was lying about it. St. Augustina already assumed they were lying to her. But spending the time to figure the mystery out wouldn't really help her current work. Let it be someone else's project. St. Augustina filed away the tip, wrapping it in a nice little package for later sale, before focusing on her current job.

St. Benedict had been caught right away. That, in itself, was as interesting as the missing body, though only to St. Augustina, since she knew the idiot personally. As much as she liked calling him that, St. Benedict wasn't much of an idiot. He was ruthless, calculating, and incredibly talented. How in the heck was he caught, and so quickly too?

There was a biotech document included in the brief. About St. Benedict. She was able to parse out a few details. One was that he was still using his ocular implants to jack into a system. While they had their advantages, she could not for the life of her understand why he hadn't simply forgone them

and gotten a jack line installed instead. They were far safer and more stable. Plus, whatever he had going on with that "wireless" marvel in his head, it had tripped the system right away. They had taken him alive.

There was nothing about the other agent.

That was where the briefing ended.

Sitting back, St. Augustina waved away the mini holodesk and pulled the ice cream sundae toward herself. The cold glass was still frosty, sending a chill down her spine as she took the first bite. Vanilla and chocolate burst across her tongue, and she sighed for a moment. When was she going to get a chance to have a good meal where all she had to do during it was eat and savor? Maybe in another life.

Right then, she needed to think. How in the world was she going to find St. Benedict? It would take a long time to hack into OverClock's network and see if she could find orders pertaining to him in their security system. She had meant it when she said she wasn't much of a hacker. She likened it to car maintenance. She could do the basics, like change a tire or the oil, but ask her to recalibrate the carburetor? She wasn't even sure that was really a thing in "car speak," and she knew even less about hacking.

Her talents had always excelled in fighting and other physical abilities, which parlayed into strategy and leadership. She was great at assembling a team, accomplishing a goal, outmaneuvering any enemy. The only thing she failed at was keeping her team alive.

Pushing those memories down, she kept her mind on the things she could control, like finding an alternate plan. A low-tech security breach was possible, as in dressing up as a maintenance worker and penetrating the old-fashioned way in search of records. But to really pull that off, time would have to pass. OverClock would be on high alert for a while, significantly decreasing her chances of entering undetected, if at all. Plus, some mild hacking might be required once she got in, and bringing in a second person would increase the chances of failure.

Yet, a second person... That got her mind going on a different tangent. Opening her mini holodesk again, she did a quick search. It seemed like almost fate when her search actually bore fruit, popping up an advertisement for a lounge act in the better part of the city.

"Of course you're around," St. Augustina muttered, as she shut down her holodesk one last time and rose from the table. Since the meal had already been paid for, St. Augustina just grabbed her goggles and gloves off the table. She slid on her long dark coat, the LED edging coming on automatically once her arms had passed through both sleeves. Staring down at the cookie jar, she hesitated a moment, then picked it up. It didn't feel like anything. Just a jar. It was just a jar.

"THANK YOU, COME AGAIN," the auto-waitress chirped as it came to collect the plates.

Out on the street, a light drizzle fell. St. Augustina pulled up her hood, the soft glow on the edge of her periphery. Slipping on her goggles, she moved down the street and over to the nearest hovercar station to get a ride across town. Being a city in the bowl of the valley, the streets themselves had been a series of switchbacks and loopy roads that tourists found bewildering, if exotic. For the locals, it made getting around impossibly long on foot.

The hovercar system almost made it manageable. Each car was built like a small bus, with seats on each side for passengers to sit and observe the glowing city below. The cars themselves hovered above the lower buildings and snaked amongst the larger buildings to various stations.

St. Augustina considered herself lucky to claim a seat, as the car was mostly full after she got on. She fell into a kind of peaceful hypnotic state as she stared out the window, watching the lights form faces and products and smiles and words above the buildings and taking none of it in.

Dammit, she was tired.

Sitting there, she felt like she hadn't rested in ages. Instead, the world around her felt more like some kind of dream. So many others were laughing and enjoying themselves, getting on and off the car, staring wide-eyed at the sights of the city, and yet none of it touched St. Augustina even as it enthralled her. She was so entranced by it all that she almost missed her stop, managing to force her way out through the bodies just before the doors shut. There was a *whoosh* at her back as the hovercar took off again, shooting into the sky mere seconds after she had exited.

The people who had gotten off before her were already filing down the long winding stairway to street level, their feet making arrhythmic tattoos on the wood-like vinyl boards of the platform and stairs. Standing under the overhang, she studied the metal curlicues decorating the edges, still beautiful despite the chipped paint.

Much on this side of town was beautiful. Once St. Augustina was on the ground, it felt like she was in a different city entirely. The lamplights were of an older style, well-maintained black-painted metal with three sconces on top throwing out yellow-colored LED light that mimicked the soft glow of oil lamps. There was little trash on the concrete. This was a street that had access to credits, still preserving a dream of prosperity without the extravagance of the truly rich. A middle-class world, one where things were simply nice.

Even the shops themselves were nice: a seamstress, a toy store, a cooking store, a gelato stand. Gelato, for god's sake! And the obvious augmentations were at a minimum in this part of town as well. LEDs still lined people's clothing, but it was subtler, many of the colors flowing with their clothes instead of looking to make a statement. Most people didn't even have their mobile devices out as they walked and talked with each other in person.

Three blocks away from the station, St. Augustina stopped in front of a brick-and-mortar building, its neon declaring it to be the Red Piano, complete with a winking woman sporting a Mary Jane-red hairstyle. A few patrons stood outside, vaping and talking in spite of the falling drizzle. St. Augustina ignored all of it and pulled open the door to step inside.

The room was awash with music paraphernalia. Even more neon lit the walls, the real stuff, highlighting records, old instruments, and various photographs that moved in three-second loops, showing everything from a big band filmed in black and white to the latest rising stars in technicolor glory. And in the air was music.

The room was as alive as an electric wire, though no one dared to speak over the dulcet tones crooning from the woman on stage. Out of everyone there, she was the most classic-looking. Dressed in a floor-length, tight-fitting, black gown, she glimmered like a black diamond in the stage lights. She wore no LEDs. Instead, old-fashioned, hand-sewn rhinestones glittered all over the gown. The old ways worked wonderfully. As for the woman herself, she parted her long blonde hair on the side, half-covering her face. A face that was the definition of sultry. Her makeup was surprisingly light, a dark tint around her eyes, and maybe the red on her lips wasn't her natural red, but it was hard to tell.

She sang like an angel.

The song sounded surprisingly familiar, though St. Augustina was hard-pressed to place it. It must have been a pop song, but the woman crooned it with such authentic emotions that it was entirely her own at that point.

As hypnotized as everyone else in the room, St. Augustina drifted up along the sidewall, coming within a few feet of the stage. She reached it just as the song ended, slipping off her goggles so she could truly see. The room erupted with claps and whooping cheers as the woman took a gracious curtsy with a dazzling smile. The piano player, who appeared to be a hologram of some generic player, twinkled down the notes of the piano. It was all for show. St. Augustina was pretty convinced now that the woman used a smart program to pipe her music through some cleverly placed speakers in the piano's body. The smart program was intuitive enough to allow some freedom of expression for the singer, following her in many of the same ways a real piano player would. Better than a recording, not quite as good as the real thing.

A fresh new chord played, signaling the start of the next song. The singer's eyes swept across her audience as she stepped up to softly rest a hand on her microphone. She missed her cue when her gaze landed on St. Augustina.

At first, St. Augustina didn't react. There was no way that the woman could see her with all those bright lights blinding her, making the audience a room of empty black faces. Yet, she kept looking at her, straight on, and she began singing right at her. It was even a song the Saint knew.

Then the woman gestured to St. Augustina as if inviting her up on stage. Double blinking, the Saint raised her hands as if to ward the woman off, shaking her head, even mouthing no at the singer's insistence. It didn't thwart the woman one bit. Taking the microphone in one manicured hand, the beautiful woman yanked it free, continuing to sing all the while. A buzz slipped through the room, and St. Augustina felt the pressure as attention began to focus on her, there at the side of the stage.

The singer's eyes seemed to laugh as she came to the edge, squatting down, which revealed the thigh-high slit in her skirt.

"St. Rachel," St. Augustina hissed at the woman, but it was too late. The microphone was between them.

Giving in to the pressure, St. Augustina joined her on the chorus, harmonizing at the perfect moment. A shiver ran through the room, and a few people cawed in delight as a few others clapped. Then the whole room cheered as St. Augustina took St. Rachel's hand and stepped up onto the stage. All St. Augustina could do was hold on to the cookie jar for dear life and sing.

While her dark clothing was wholly inappropriate next to the glitter of St. Rachel's dress, she soon forgot about it, swept away on the notes and the approval of the crowd. She even got daring as her voice warmed up, meeting St. Rachel's amused eyes before hitting a grace note flourish.

St. Rachel didn't release her hand once they got up there together. Instead, once she had replaced the microphone, she grasped her prisoner's fingers and laced them with her own. Looking at each other, they nodded in time as the song approached its end, the music between them buzzing in perfect harmony with each other.

The last note played, and then silence.

Then the room roared. The cheers and whistles cut through it, making the cacophony sound more like an avalanche than applause. St. Rachel pulled St. Augustina in for a hug, the cookie jar squashed between them, and in that moment, the other Saint was her only anchor in the world to hold on to.

"Follow me," St. Rachel said in her ear, then she turned with that beatific smile. "Thank you! Thank you, everyone, for coming out tonight," she said, adding more platitudes as they made their way toward the edge of the stage. She poignantly had not mentioned St. Augustina's name, for which the Saint was grateful, even if it was bad decorum.

"That was fantastic!" someone said as they went down the small flight of steps off to the side. St. Augustina forced a smile and nodded as others echoed the praise.

St. Rachel never let her go as she elegantly moved through the crowd, never pushing them out of the way, but definitely deflecting her way past them toward a single black door just next to the bar. A woman at the bar handed each of them a full martini glass as another person opened the door for them to pass through. Only at that point did they step in to block the patrons from following the two women, cutting off the cacophony abruptly with the slam of the door.

"Oh, thank God!" St. Rachel exclaimed once the door was shut, and she had drunk down half of the contents of the glass. "I have more of this in my room," she added as she saluted with the glass, then led the way down the cluttered hallway. The hall was quite narrow and treacherous, lined with props, lights, and many of the typical things one expected to find in the backroom of a bar.

Turning a corner, St. Rachel shoved her hip against a thick door and entered a dressing room. Or, at least half of it was a dressing room. The other half was still being used for storage.

The minute the women crossed the threshold, St. Rachel kicked off her heels. The shiny, black shoes winked as they sailed to land on top of the storage bins.

"Come in, we have a lot to talk about," St. Rachel said, going straight to the mirror on the dressing table, bending over to click on the lights that framed it. Retrieving a bottle from a drawer, she refreshed her drink and held the bottle out to St. Augustina, who was still juggling the glass, the cookie jar, and closing the door.

"Let me get a first drink in!" St. Augustina chided, using the door to support her weight as she took a taste from her glass. The dusty sweetness hit her tongue, followed by a little bit of a kick as she swallowed. "Damn," St. Augustina muttered.

"Ages since you had a good Manhattan, huh?" St. Rachel asked bemused.

"Ages and ages," St. Augustina agreed.

"You going to hold the door open all night?"

"I can't believe you did that to me," St. Augustina chided, then took a proper drink from her glass.

"I was planning it the whole time, ever since I was told you were coming."

"Who told you I was coming?"

"Who do you think? Nice to actually be doing a job *with* you for a change." St. Rachel slid some clothes off a movie director's folding chair, and St. Augustina headed toward it.

"Wait, would you unhook my back?" St. Rachel asked, just as St. Augustina was passing, turning to show her bare back, except for the single hook at the top behind her neck. Setting the drink on the corner of the dressing table and the cookie jar on the floor, it was still a bit of a fumble trying to undo the clasp with gloves, but St. Rachel continued chatting as she waited. "I'm actually surprised you agreed to help find St. Benedict. What did the Orange Lady offer you to convince you?" St. Rachel asked.

"A cookie jar."

St. Rachel laughed as she stepped away, letting her dress drop. She wore only a black pair of panties underneath. Her body was as perfect as her face. Yet, St. Rachel was the one who turned around and appraised her.

"You look good."

St. Augustina shrugged, taking a seat in the director's folding chair. "I'm alive."

"Still a far cry from those powersuits you usually wear."

"I wear what's required for the job," she answered, feeling rather badass as she crossed her ankle over her knee, her knee-high, reinforced combat boots on full display. She watched St. Rachel's eyes pass over them admiringly, even as she slipped into a beautiful silky robe that made her look like a honey bunny. St. Rachel's sex appeal was her greatest weapon, but St. Augustina knew that deep down, the other Saint was a fighter like her. Driving a fist through an asshole's face was her drug of choice.

Unfortunately, the Deacons took one lustful look at her face and body and augmented her to fulfill any target's desires. Therefore, she lacked the reinforcement and mechanical assistance in the joints and bones that made St. Augustina harder to break and stronger than a truck. It had been one of the few choices the Deacons had offered St. Augustina, beauty or brawn. St. Rachel, they just *did* it to her. It created sympathy within her for the other Saint.

She couldn't call St. Rachel a friend; none of the Saints could ever truly be friends with each other, considering their training and missions often pitted them against each other. Yet, if she were to give anyone the term, it would be St. Rachel.

"What is your take on this mission?" St. Augustina asked, taking another sip from her glass, wondering if it was wise and if she cared to get a refill from whatever St. Rachel's bottle held.

"Seems straightforward to me. Rescue St. Ben, use his codes to crack that thing open, we all go out to lunch. Why? What's your take?"

"What if we just leave St. Benedict out of it?"

That made St. Rachel pause. A shocked look passed over her face, then a calculating one to St. Augustina's relief. A Saint always calculated the odds; it was a part of the programming. If she weren't at all willing to toss St. Benedict to the wayside for their mission, St. Augustina would have thought this whole thing was actually a twisted setup between the two of them. Or, possibly, St. Rachel represented an unknown third party that would not want them to abandon an asset like St. Benedict.

"How would we get into the canister?" St. Rachel asked.

Picking up the cookie jar, which rattled as if there was something actually inside it, St. Augustina sighed and looked down at the locks.

"From what I can deduce, each of these locks are actually programs. You are a better hacker than I; surely we can break some programming together?"

"It was the first thing I tried," St. Rachel lied smoothly. St. Augustina almost didn't catch it, she had gotten much, much better at it. So had St. Augustina. Now the radar was back up. St. Rachel *was* hiding something, something about the digital cookie jar and its magical locks. Mentally, she snorted at her joke. If only magic really did exist, she could just say the magic words and get this mystery jar to open.

"Alright, I'll take that on *faith* then. Do you know where he is?" St. Augustina replied, not even checking to see if her subtle barb sank in or not.

The other Saint laughed as she pulled on a black sports bra. "Yes, of course. I swear half of my life is dedicated to bailing him out of trouble."

"Still pining after him, then?"

St. Rachel's eyes sparked daggers, even as her mask and voice remained smiling. "We all have our price." She turned away and pulled a set of dark clothes from the bottom of an open suitcase by the dressing table. "What is your problem with St. Benedict anyway? You guys disappeared on a mission the best of partners and came back with a blood vendetta between you."

"He betrayed me. I took exception to that."

Rolling her eyes, St. Rachel slipped on black combat pants similar to St. Augustina's. "We're Saints. Loyalty is the only thing we can't have. You shouldn't take it personally."

"We weren't Saints then."

"Ha, yes, we were. We both know it was a statistical miracle we survived that at all." She went still as her eyes drifted to a place in the past that St. Augustina could see as well. "All of them. We were all Saints, even the ones who fell."

"You really believe that?" St. Augustina asked, her voice barely above a whisper.

"I have to. I still have to live with myself," St. Rachel said, smiling weakly before slipping on a black ninja shirt, wrapping the ends tight around her shapely form.

While watching her, St. Augustina rolled what St. Rachel said in her mind. "It's not that I'm taking it personally..."

"What exactly happened then?"

In her mind's eye, St. Augustina saw the moment when she realized that St. Benedict had turned on her to survive. It had been a real mission with real stakes. Penetrate a drug cartel's inner-city connection, steal certain data from the office computer, return to base. A very basic mission that usually took a solid team of eight to ten to pull off.

It was just the two of them, and it was terrifying.

If she had been teamed with anyone other than St. Benedict, she was certain the mission would have failed. Yet, he had a way of making her believe they could beat the odds. And she had believed, up until it came to their escape. They needed more time for their route to open up, diamond cutters drilling through the thick metal walls. So, he shoved her out the door of the vault and slammed it shut behind her, counting on her to fight, even if she was hopelessly outnumbered, giving him enough time to escape.

She remembered screaming as she pummeled the door with the butt of her stolen rifle, "Why?! Why?!"

He didn't even look at her through the clear, shatterproof plastic of the door.

In that moment, she knew why. She hadn't understood what he had meant when he said he would do whatever it took to survive. He had been comforting her at the time, after she told him she had decided to simply let the Deacons kill her in the next simulation. That she couldn't take it anymore. St. Cornelius had gone that way only hours prior. Just simply stood there and let the bullets tear through him. It seemed a quick, easy way to escape the pain, fear, and never-ending suffering.

He had told her not to give up, that she could make it. There was hope on the other side that she would see her parents again. That was the night she first thought she could trust him. He told her he would do whatever it took to survive and why. He told St. Augustina about *her*. Not her name, but someone he loved. He spoke of small precious details about her, so clear that they were fused in St. Augustina's mind, so much so that she began to believe it herself. She began to believe that if she stuck with him, she would make it out too.

Except, the truth was, she was a resource to be sacrificed instead of a friend.

"He killed my hope."

"You were the last of us to lose it," St. Rachel said, soberly, as she plaited her own hair into a crown around her head.

"No. He was," St. Augustina countered bitterly.

"Now, I don't know about that. I would argue he was the first to lose it. It was gone before he entered the program, that's for sure. What he had was his mission. That's not the same as having hope."

"When did you lose hope?" St. Augustina asked, looking at St. Rachel's reflection in the mirror.

St. Rachel didn't respond. Instead, she stood up and slipped a black cap over her blonde hair. "Are you ready?"

"No, I have one more question before I walk out that door with you," St. Augustina said, leaning back in the chair as if she intended to stay there, maybe order another drink.

"Then ask it," the other Saint said coolly, slipping into the femme fatale persona that she wore so well.

"Why are you here, St. Rachel?"

She blinked as if she had been expecting a different question. Maybe she had. Still, St. Augustina waited, her face blank and expectant.

"Because..." The femme fatale mask slipped and St. Rachel looked down, almost shyly. "I wanted to help you." Lifting her head, she locked eyes with St. Augustina, actual tears standing in them. "Because I can."

St. Augustina swallowed. She didn't trust that. She couldn't afford to, but she couldn't make herself doubt St. Rachel's sincerity. "Saints don't just do favors for anybody. Especially other Saints."

Nervously, St. Augustina fiddled with one of the locks, and it came away in her hands. She stared at it as if it was a piece of her own body that had randomly fallen off.

"Oh," St. Rachel said as well, her eyes wide. "Well, that's convenient."

Turning the lock around in her hands, St. Augustina studied it. It was a very different lock from the others. Black in body with a plastic-like texture. The lock bit was braided metal instead of a bent bar. There was no dial or key slot. Yet, her fingers found grooves in the underside. Turning it in toward the bright lights surrounding St. Rachel's dressing table, she saw five straight lines and two bars of notes printed on the bottom.

"Oh, wow," St. Rachel breathed, leaning sideways to see, but not block the light.

St. Augustina replaced the tabbed end of the lock. "You take the high; I'll take the harmony." It took a minute to figure out the starting key, but once they had finished singing, the lock popped open on its own.

"It must have unlocked while we were singing," St. Rachel said, taking the lock from St. Augustina to look at herself.

"Did you know?" St. Augustina asked, trying to puzzle it out.

St. Rachel shook her head.

"You simply happened to pick a song that would be the key to opening the lock," St. Augustina countered with hooded eyes.

St. Rachel handed the lock back. "Look, if I was a part of some under-handed conspiracy to trick you, I would just tell you because it would definitely save us a lot of trouble."

If she was lying, St. Augustina couldn't detect it. Instead, she opened her mini holodesk and set the lock on the desktop. "That's eerie," she muttered as the lock simply sat there, then disappeared with the desktop as she dismissed it.

"Augmented reality," St. Rachel shrugged, plucking up a mask from a blank mannequin. "It's a whole new world."

"Then let's get going before they stick us into a museum as collectors' pieces."

CHAPTER 6

The alleyway across town was relatively empty, at least in comparison with the main streets. After maneuvering amongst the crush of bodies and carts of the darker part of the city, the two Saints were able to walk side by side more easily now. Maybe a half dozen others stood in a small group halfway down, vaping in a circle. Two more were making out and fornicating between two dumpsters.

"Yeah, give it to her, Calvin!" one from the group hollered to the laughter of the others.

"Of course, his name's Calvin. When isn't it a Calvin?" St. Augustina muttered as they continued past.

"What's wrong with Calvins?" St. Rachel asked.

"Never met one who wasn't an egotistical player, big man for his britches." St. Augustina's steps began to slow, though. Something about the name tickled her brain. Something she both did and did not want to remember...

"Ignore them," St. Rachel said, as she fixed the mask over her face and closed it with a click. The click snapped St. Augustina back to the task at hand, and they continued.

The group vaping were obviously kitchen staff drawing out their breaks as long as they could. St. Augustina kept an eye on them in her goggles' rearviews, but the group didn't even spare a glance for the pair. She supposed the Saints were too alien a sight, best to be avoided and better forgotten.

While St. Augustina had her goggles on and hood up, St. Rachel wore a full-face cover, something akin to a stylized version of an air raid mask. It was outfitted much like St. Augustina's, with rear cameras and enhanced audio, enabling St. Rachel to be more aware than she would be with just her natural or even augmented senses. Plus, it had the added effect of being intimidating. She also sported a hood, pulled up over the black cap that hid her blonde hair.

They had been inadvertently trailing a couple up ahead of them. Both were dressed in too-fashionable-to-be-authentic stylish clothing, the woman draped over the man's arm in such a way that made it obvious she was on something. Probably a mob man and his "lady for the night," clearly heading to the same place the Saints were heading. The Underground, a burlesque strip club/techno bordello. An every-fantasy-being-fulfilled kind of place.

Naturally, when the marks they were following stopped, St. Rachel and St. Augustina paused, their hidden eyes making it possible to observe them without seeming like they were doing anything at all. The mobster man rapped at the door of The Underground with an honest-to-god gold cane while his lady friend giggled like a pig. A slot opened in the door, and he stuck his hand through so fast it was obvious he was trying to prove how daring he was. The door opened for them, and the couple disappeared.

"*You ready?*" St. Rachel's voice asked directly in St. Augustina's ear. They had synced before they had left the lounge, the closest thing to telepathy that technology had achieved.

"*If you trust your guy, then I'm ready,*" St. Augustina said, touching her R-pistol under her coat to reassure herself that it was unhooked and ready for a quick draw if need be. The Underground was invitation only. Paying the right price for an invitation was tricky, even on a low-stakes night.

Together they approached the door. St. Augustina rapped at it as soon as it was within reach, while St. Rachel nonchalantly checked their immediate surroundings.

"Obviously, there is a camera above the door, but I sense two others across the street," St. Rachel reported.

"Good, then we're in the right place. I have no patience for a copy-cat operation."

She raised her fist to rap again, but St. Rachel stopped it.

"Don't. You're only allowed one chance to knock."

"Nice idiot test," St. Augustina said, nodding. "Not that I'm questioning your plan, but isn't there an easier way for us to jack in?

"If it was just you and me, probably, but it isn't just you and me, so we're going to need a pirated setup. Besides, OverClock's parent company will be monitoring all company-approved setups."

"I'm not suggesting that we use a trademarked setup. I'm saying there must have been other options."

"Like I said, if it was only us, then yes."

"Who else...?"

The slot finally opened in the door, cutting off St. Augustina's thought. St. Rachel stuck her hand in, igniting her hand augmentation to project the invitation once it was inside. There was undefined movement on the other side of the door, and St. Augustina hoped it was the doorkeeper verifying their invite, not preparing to cut off St. Rachel's hand. Schrödinger's trap.

The door opened, and St. Augustina released the breath she hadn't realized she had been holding.

An androgynous person held the door open, their eyes covered by slitted glasses with a small light regularly blinking on the corner of the frame.

"Come on, let's go," they said, gesturing with a clipboard. The Saints entered, and the door shut with the musical boom of finality. The three of them stood in a dark, dank utility hallway, bathed in green light from a metal-guarded sconce above.

The androgynous person opened a clear bin on a small conveyer belt, removing a tab from the top. "All weapons in here, please. They will be returned to you at the end of your visit. You will be scanned after you have disarmed yourselves. All those who comply voluntarily and pass the scan get free drink tokens good for this event only. Thank you for your compliance," they said with a rote air.

Without hesitation, St. Augustina dropped her R-gun and laser knife in the bin, knowing she probably wasn't getting them back. The price of the job. In truth, if she needed a weapon in there, she would be able to acquire one from someone else. As movie cliché as it may have sounded, *she* was the weapon.

St. Rachel dropped her own pair of laser knives into the bin, along with a steel knife and a small-caliber exceller-gun. The androgynous person handed St. Augustina a tab, with the number T691 on it in flaming black.

"We are augmented," St. Rachel said, the mask she wore warping her voice into gravel and at least an octave lower.

"Oh, great," the androgynous person said, not at all impressed or concerned. They waved the Saints both to step through a second door. It turned out to be a small chamber, just large enough for two people. On the floor were the outlines of two sets of footprints next to each other. "Place your feet on the marks indicated and raise your hands to the ceiling. This will take only a few seconds." Then they shut the door. There was a hum, and the sound of air decompressing before a curved wand embedded in the wall of the chamber whipped around twice. St. Augustina didn't feel anything, but the wand must have done its job because the door on the other side of the chamber opened.

A shorter woman with a spikey mohawk and LED ear-loops gestured them out. "Please wait here a moment," she said.

They did just that, standing in awkward silence for what seemed like ages. The short woman even gave them an anxious smile as the wait dragged on. Both Saints stayed completely still, waiting to learn if this was a fight-or-flight situation. Hopefully, their intimidating appearances would give them a solid edge against the telegraphing doorkeeper. St. Augustina pitied her, even knowing that if that light didn't come out right, the shorter woman would be obligated to try to subdue them, probably in an any-means-necessary kind of way. The woman knew she was door fodder, someone too low in the organization to warrant much concern if any of the darker elements coming into the club decided to retribute against her.

Then a blue light dinged next to the short woman, and her shoulders slumped in relief. "Okay, flash these wristbands at the bar and they'll serve you," she said, whipping out two glowing bands flashing between pink and green. "Don't lose them. They will not be replaced." She moved to fasten them on their wrists, but St. Rachel didn't hold out her hand, and the shorter woman hesitated, uncertain.

"*St. Rachel, stop scaring her,*" St. Augustina said through their link.

"*Oh my god, she's adorable,*" St. Rachel replied, then held out her wrist. The short woman did her task with shaking fingers, then did St. Augustina's.

"Down the hall at the end. When you wish to leave, there is an exit on the other side of the main room. You will be able to reclaim your things there. Ha-have a good time!" she tried to say cheerily.

The Saints turned away and proceeded the way they'd been directed without another word. If they had said anything more, the woman probably would have peed herself.

There was a low thumping as they approached the end of the hall. A pair of metal double doors opened on their own once the pair approached. The thumping became louder as club music poured out.

The room itself had a good-sized crowd meandering around a thrust stage. LEDs flashed alternating colors while defused light from mirrored chandeliers threw faerie light across the ceiling. There seemed to be all kinds in attendance, from wealthy CEOs and playboys or girls to the underworld's monsters of note and everyone in between. Most people were like them, making a token effort to hide their identities, though the ones that insisted on being served versus going up to the room-length bar to order their drinks, gave themselves away. Most people had the same wristbands as the Saints, which meant they too had passed the weapon-free test.

St. Rachel moved toward the bar, and people gave them a decent berth.

"*The mask seems to be doing its job,*" St. Augustina said, continuing to survey the room as St. Rachel claimed some real estate to place their order. "*You should walk around like this all the time.*"

"Not surprised. I mean, look at this. Don't I look sexy?" St. Rachel laughed.

"I'm sure there is someone out there who would be into it," St. Augustina replied, unable to keep the amusement out of her voice.

"Only it's not working too well on these bartenders," she said and slapped her hand on the bar to get some attention.

While St. Rachel negotiated for service, St. Augustina focused on the layout of the room. Like the doorwoman had said, there was a second set of double doors on the opposite end with a blue neon sign declaring it the exit. A dozen neutrally suited people were wandering around with earpieces in, their blandness declaring themselves security. So, if anyone picked a fight, they would be instantly fighting a battle on multiple fronts.

Six others moved about the room with tablets, taking orders and making arrangements. These folks were dressed minimally; St. Augustina couldn't shake the feeling she had seen their too-sexy outfits recently, but she couldn't place where. It was as if someone had used materials from a construction site and tried to design clothing out of them.

They were obviously the concierge service. The Saints were going to have to snag a service provider soon to claim a room that had both a jack-in set up and a VR set up for the mysterious third person St. Rachel kept alluding to. All of them kept more or less near the thrust stage that almost completely bisected the room.

On the thrust, currently, was a couple of sexual practitioners preparing to demonstrate what manner of fantasies were possible once a patron chose to reserve and pay for a room. These live shows were more of a demonstration to get people's "juices" flowing since most encounters would be happening virtually instead of in RL. Still, the showings of whatever product was being highlighted that day often were worth the price of admission in and of itself.

A couple of young men in fancy suits and obviously already drunk kept daring each other to touch the stage, getting shocked by the edging that kept too-eager hands away from the merchandise. It was more for show than actual harm because if she really wanted to, St. Augustina could make it up on that stage with little to no ill effect.

"Extraction is going to be messy if things go wrong," St. Augustina said.

"Are you concerned?"

"Yes, I'm not stupid. Too many things could go wrong."

"We don't have the resources to locate him the old-fashioned way or bust him out action-movie style if we did. This will be far more efficient. I thought you would appreciate that."

"I do," St. Augustina conceded. There was an elegance to St. Rachel's plan. Greasing the right palms had garnered the needed information that OverClock had decided they preferred to make an example, and a profit, off their catch and had sold off St. Benedict to a chop shop.

It was as gruesome as it sounded.

Body parts for sale, to the highest bidder, guaranteed fresh on the spot. Augmentations had come a long way, but in some respect, nothing replaced what nature had created. Especially with all the pharmaceutical advancements that made rejection basically nonexistent.

Luckily for St. Benedict, OverClock obviously didn't understand what they had, and whoever was running the chop shop did. Just because nature had a vintage ascetic that people liked, didn't mean you chopped up a Ferrari when you could get more from selling the whole. Skills and education were not something that came with the meaty bits individually but could be just as valuable. Hence the word-of-mouth announcement on the right chat spaces about an auction of whole people up for sale. And if the Ferrari didn't sell, then chop-chop.

St. Augustina sighed. "He's definitely not worth all this trouble."

"*Which is why we're going to bid on him,*" her temporary partner replied, handing over a cold, brown bottle.

"You have the funds if this goes how I'd expect?"

"Huh, there are pockets that will be watching this auction that are so deep, both of us would drown in them."

"Then what's your plan?"

"What else? Sniping."

St. Augustina chuffed a dry laugh. "*We won't be the only ones doing that.*"

"We will be the only ones with my abilities doing it," St. Rachel said, confidently.

Even though St. Augustina heard St. Rachel's answer, she didn't really register it. Her focus was centered on the last figure she expected to see there.

Across the room, sitting in a chair on the opposite side of the stage, was the Orange Lady. She was bedecked as she had been in the diner, in orange light, but instead of a skintight body suit, her dress was layers of orange patterned cloth that seemed to hover around her form. It was unclear how the fabric maintained a dress shape, as it didn't seem to be held together with any visible stitches or hooks. Rather, the pattern seemed to flow and move around her body like a slow-moving river. Though she wasn't standing, her feet were festooned in some impossible orange stilettos with three balls of LED lights flashing in a seemingly random sequence. Her hair was coiffed up in a sweeping sea of braids with other balls of orange light coiled up into it.

"*Do you see her?*" St. Augustina asked, grabbing St. Rachel's wrist. Keeping her eyes on the Orange Lady, she waited for the other Saint to spot their supposed employer.

"*Good, she's here. We can put our reservation in,*" St. Rachel said, taking a drink from a martini glass.

The lights shifted in the room at that moment. The patrons began to redistribute as those from the bar moved to both sides of the runway. Some took chairs, but many remained standing in the back, along with the two Saints.

No one said a word, as the music grew louder, a heavy bass thumping a clear indication of the expected rhythms to come. The performers on the stage began their show.

St. Augustina didn't really see it. Her focus was on the Orange Lady.

"Keeping an eye on her investments?" St. Augustina asked, coolly, feeling annoyed.

"I hate being micromanaged as much as you do, but here we are. She wants to be involved in getting our hands on St. Benedict, and I'm not really in a position to argue with her. We are her team. I wouldn't be involved in any of this if it wasn't for St. Benedict," St. Rachel said airily in her mind as if the inevitable tragedy wasn't worth getting upset over.

"Title of your autobiography," St. Augustina thought before she remembered that even casual thoughts could be transmitted via the link between them.

"Yes. Thank you for that," St. Rachel said and went back to her drink, which she consumed via a black straw through the breathing hole in her mask.

St. Augustina knew St. Rachel wasn't sharing all the details, but it irritated her that her temporary partner was playing it a little too casually. It wasn't like St. Augustina was some amateur who couldn't see through what St. Rachel was doing, even if she still wasn't sure why. There really wasn't much St. Augustina could do about it, and what was really important at that moment was finishing her part of the job. There was a reason she was the one keeping the cookie jar safe.

Swallowing the bile in her throat, St. Augustina chased it with the beer St. Rachel had given her. It bit in all the right ways and refocused her.

A concierge finally passed close enough, and she snagged his attention. He gave a little start when he saw their masks but mustered some professionalism enough to smile.

"How can I serve you today?"

"Room for three," St. Rachel's modulated voice growled out.

"Ah, yes, I see." The concierge began tapping at his tablet. "Any special modifications required?"

"Two jack-in chairs and a cap."

The concierge's fingers paused over the tablet a moment as he took that information in. "I'm sorry, but we don't have..."

St. Rachel passed her augmented hand over his tablet. It changed something St. Augustina couldn't clearly see on the screen. The concierge's eyes widened a moment as he read whatever was there, then nodded. "I see. Yes, that changes..." he began tapping quickly.

"What did you do?" St. Augustina thought at her temporary partner.

"What else? I bribed him."

"I have exactly what you require. Please give me a moment to have it prepared. Will you need anything else? Can I have a private bar and meal service set up for you?"

"That would be nice," St. Augustina said since it had been a few hours since she had last eaten. He nodded and walked off, his focus still absorbed in his tablet.

The show on the stage ended, and the whole event proceeded to the next without much other fanfare.

"You don't seem happy to see me?" The Orange Lady appeared next to the Saints as the stage was cleared, preparing to reset. The patrons were meandering again, giving the trio some natural space.

"If you were going to come with us in the first place, why didn't you come with me from the diner?" St. Augustina asked plainly.

"I had other preparations to make, as did you. I did say I would see you later." She smiled broadly, looking as gorgeous as a princess. Too bad this wasn't a folk tale. And St. Augustina wasn't allowed to punch her. The Orange Lady cocked her head to the side. "I don't think you like me very much."

"I don't like not knowing the plan."

That only made the Orange Lady smile broader.

"We've reserved a room," St. Rachel interjected, her voice modulator failing to mask her obvious anxiousness.

"*Dammit, St. Rachel, even when you're supposed to be undercover you are sucking up to the boss,*" St. Augustina hissed in her mind, not really caring that St. Rachel could hear her. It was easy to imagine St. Rachel's covered eyes narrowing at her.

"Your room is ready," the concierge cut in, approaching the group to offer a solicitous arm toward a far door.

St. Augustina became aware that the tone of the room had changed. It seemed almost sinister as a curl of blackened smoke wafted over the door as the next act came out. A tall, broad man made of defined muscle had taken the stage, wearing blue jeans and very little else. His head was bowed, and his hands were clasped behind his back, making his shoulders pop out. The room was screaming and cheering, showing something very different from the dark, near-silent lust of the previous show.

"Something is wrong," St. Augustina muttered under her breath.

"St. Augustina?" St. Rachel asked out loud, turning toward her as St. Augustina continued to back up out of the pressing crowd. More smoke filled the space, making it harder and harder to see and hear or breathe.

"We need... we need to get..." There was a trumpeting, a sound caught between a scream and a whinny. St. Augustina's veins went ice cold as a memory threatened to surface, something that she would be safer forgetting. The trumpeting digitized and warped into a screeching beat.

Her attention caught as if in a trap, St. Augustina watched the man on the stage lift his blonde head. Antlers.

Furrowing her brows, she tore the goggles down from her face so she could see clearer. That was wrong. It wasn't supposed to be antlers. A stag man? He began to dance, bucking his head and letting the roll slink down his body fluidly. The motion seemed to free St. Augustina, and she proceeded to back up again, even if she couldn't look away. Not until the Orange Lady stepped between them.

"St. Augustina. Idrina," she said, forcing the Saint to tear her gaze away. "Focus on me, child. You must let it go. Whatever you fear, you must let it go now, or you will summon it to you."

"No..." St. Augustina whimpered. The miasmic smoke curled around the teeny-bopper's shoulders, suppressing the light of her LEDs. Soon she would be consumed like the rest of the room was. Yet, the Orange Lady didn't seem to be affected by it.

"You must focus. Let go of what you fear," she repeated, squeezing St. Augustina's arm and smiling. The music was fading, swallowed by the darkness. Where was she? Her retreat had been stopped by a lone, black tree, its bark biting into her skin as her hand scrabbled against it, scraping bloodlessly along her knuckles.

"I can't," St. Augustina cried.

"Why?"

"Because... because..." she started to say, her heart thumping, telling her to run.

"What would your mother say in the face of this darkness?"

"What?" St. Augustina blinked at the question, the gun rattling in her hand. Her mother?

"She was a soldier, yes? She must have faced great dangers and felt fear countless times. A parent would share the wisdom learned from such encounters. What did she say to you when you were afraid?"

"She said..." St. Augustina saw her mother emerge out of the thick smoky darkness surrounding her, the image of her dressed as she had been from St. Augustina's favorite picture, standing in front of her chopper. Her mother had been more than a soldier. She had been a warrior.

"Bravery," St. Augustina whispered, hearing her mother's voice as she spoke, "isn't the absence of fear."

"What is it?" the Orange Lady asked, matching her whisper.

"It is the belief that something else is more important than fear."

The thick smoke dissipated as the music came back. The people all around them were jumping and screeching in Bacchic revelry as the man on the stage gyrated his hips in one woman's face. Thin, white smoke spurted into the air from the edges of the stage. No one noticed the little drama happening by the near-empty bar. St. Rachel stood beside her, a hand holding her shoulder, her head cocked to the side in concern. St. Augustina imagined that if she really could see the Saint's face through the mask, it would look worried.

"Are you alright now?" St. Rachel asked out loud.

"Don't mention it anymore," the Orange Lady corrected, taking St. Augustina's hand to lead her out of the room. "We need to focus on the task at hand."

"Right," St. Augustina said, nodding as if stunned. She wanted to ask what happened, but also seemed to know that was a bad, bad idea. Whatever had just happened could wait until later. "We have something more important to do right now."

CHAPTER 7

"This will make you lose your faith in humanity," St. Rachel said, her musical voice restored after taking the mask off once they got to their room.

"These people certainly have lost it." St. Augustina continued to scroll through the listing. They were sitting at an old-fashioned console computer, staring at a list on the screen. There were very few actual names on the list. Mostly what was given was some descriptor title to make the living merchandise sound somewhat appealing. Like bio-scientist, car mechanic woman, hot blond, etc. Once you clicked through, a page popped up that had more details organized in a fillable form. It began with a list of skills or natural qualities, as well as a list of available body parts, blood types, and overall health. If you wanted a new name, you could scroll down to the bottom where you could buy a new identity. There was even an "identity plus" option, which included a bio-chip implant, new fingertips, and dental records. It all had to come from somewhere, though, and it often came from the people society misplaced.

"Why don't they have a search function?" St. Rachel complained.

"The better to prosecute you with, my dear?" St. Augustina guessed as she continued to scroll through the names, scanning for keywords that might be St. Benedict. "This is an incredibly illegal and temporary operation. Most of this product won't even be here tomorrow, so why bother setting up a keyword search?"

"I know that," St. Rachel replied, surly, "I still want one."

To be honest, St. Augustina did too.

Truthfully, they were lucky to find this website. Even with it being in the deep web, three other websites St. Augustina had known about had been raided, taken, or simply destroyed to preempt a raid. If St. Augustina hadn't noticed the floating icon in the back of the main error screen, they wouldn't have found this new link to the current page.

"Oh, crap. There are children on here," St. Rachel said, sounding sick.

"Try not to think about it. We can send this new link to the authorities if you like when we're done. Call it our good deed for the day," St. Augustina said, firmly burying her own sick feeling. She couldn't save all of them, and she wasn't even sure the authorities would either. "It's not the mission."

"It could be," the Orange Lady said from behind them.

St. Rachel shot her a look over their shoulders. "No, it couldn't be."

"Okay, how about this one? Obnoxious loud mouth."

Clicking the link popped up a live video of a balding, sallow-looking older man. "There... there is no justice to be found here," the scientist gasped out. If his disdain had been a poison, it would have melted those who viewed his suffering dispassionately, or at least melted away the dispassionate camera that was watching him. "Only the darkness remains, there is no light. The world beyond us is waiting, but we can never reach it. The unicorn..."

"Okay, just a crazy guy." St. Augustina clicked off the viewscreen. "Not our crazy guy."

"Maybe they know what he is, and they aren't going to put him up for sale," the Orange Lady said.

"Or we're at the wrong online auction," St. Rachel said.

Letting her fingers hover over the real keyboard, a thought hit St. Augustina. "Or we're looking in the wrong place," she concluded and started tapping furiously.

A new list appeared.

"Currently on auction? We already looked there."

"Sometimes these sites have a VIP section," St. Augustina said, clicking on a small golden rubber duckie icon at the corner of the screen. A password box popped up.

St. Rachel pushed away from the desk. "Okay, I'm going to have to jack in to run the password-hacking software."

The Orange Lady stopped her. "Where is the cookie jar?" she asked.

The Saints exchanged a glance. "Safe. Why?" St. Augustina asked.

"This universe had been trying to tell you something if only you would listen," the Orange Lady said, sagely.

"I highly doubt the cookie jar has the password for a human auction site." Then St. Augustina narrowed her eyes. "Unless there is a reason it would."

"There is a reason for everything, everywhere. We may not always be able to discern the pattern. But..." the Orange Lady swallowed, "for some reason, you seem to be the center of this..." and then the teeny-bopper looked down, "thing... happening here."

There it was.

"You have five seconds to confess whatever setup this is before I simply kill you and walk away," St. Augustina stated. She had had enough of all of these convenient coincidences. Especially because the Orange Lady was right. They all seemed to center around herself. Who was doing this to her? What was really going on? This thin lie that they really didn't know what was going on was breaking apart, and St. Augustina was going to get the answers she needed right now.

"You think this is some sort of conspiracy against you personally, St. Augustina?" St. Rachel said, standing up behind her. St. Augustina thought she could feel the heat of the hand the other Saint didn't dare lay on her shoulder. "If that were true, it would have to be the work of another Saint."

"What makes you say that?" St. Augustina questioned darkly, though her own mind was already calculating how that could be true, and it was starting to make sense.

"Who else could work like that? Think of the cookie jar. Didn't you say it looks exactly like one your grandmother used to have?"

St. Augustina made a gesture and summoned her holodesk. Sitting in the middle of it was the cookie jar and its belt of locks. She flinched when she stared at it. There had been only two locks undone, now there were three. Reaching out, she brought the jar out and slid off the unlocked lock. It had been an alphabet lock that now spelled "bravery."

"What. The. Hell. Is. Going. On," St. Augustina said softly, her tongue feeling like she had swallowed dust. The cookie jar felt like a ten-pound weight in her hands, despite its non-existence.

"Someone is targeting you with this," St. Rachel stated. "Someone created that around you. You're the key to answering all the locks: your life, your experiences. They made you the lock."

"What's in the cookie jar?" St. Augustina demanded.

The Orange Lady's eyes widened larger; near panic, she took a wobbling step backward on her ridiculous heels. "I..." She looked to St. Rachel for help, but none was forthcoming. "I was told... it has secrets pertaining to the Saints."

"What do you want to do with the secrets of the Saints?" St. Augustina asked the Orange Lady, the fingers from her other hand slipping up to grasp her Saint Box.

"To undo them," the Orange Lady stated. "To find the answer to freeing the Saints from their traps."

"Why?"

"Does it matter why? Do we really have time to mess with this?" St. Rachel asked, taking the cookie jar from St. Augustina. She turned it in her hands a moment until she came around to a lock. It was flat, but distinctly shaped and shaded gold like the stylized rubber ducky icon from the website. Across its body was the word "Poh."

"What the hell is POH?" St. Rachel asked, lifting up the lock to read it.

"A dark creature from the far east," the Orange Lady said, ominously.

"It's obviously an acronym," St. Augustina muttered, heading for the computer.

"Does it eat people?" St. Rachel asked, sarcastically.

"Among other things."

Not wasting any more time, St. Augustina returned to the keyboard and typed POH into the password bar. It only spun for a second, then the plain white wallpaper on the website refreshed itself with a gold duck pattern. At the same time, the ducky lock clicked open.

"What the hell?" St. Augustina whispered, looking back and forth between the jar and the screen.

"We'll figure it out later. Look!" St. Rachel said, pointing a gloved finger at the screen.

There was a live video playing. It was St. Benedict. He stood on a sort of stage with a line-up of other people. They were being presented one by one.

It looked like the first few of the lot had been brought forward, a bio-scientist and some sort of engineer. Both were obviously stolen from their company research labs along with their transfer papers, which the MC held up as he talked about their credentials. After a moment, listing off words that St. Augustina flatly did not understand, he gestured them back, trading papers with a woman dressed like an assistant on a game show, except one with ratings falling as fast as her plunging neckline.

The MC himself was a piece of work too, dressed in black mesh cut into the shape of a suit. Underneath, he seemed to be wearing tight neon underwear and matching body paint, or possibly tattoos, striping up his sides and down the outsides of his arms.

Smiling a too-perfect smile of white, very even teeth, he brought the third lot forward and proceeded to read from the new set of papers he had received.

"If we want to be able to pull this bid-sniping off, we need to get in there," St. Augustina said, dropping the cookie jar and its mysteries back into her holodesk, shutting it off, then going to one of the lounge chairs. It smelled of cleaner, and the over-dried leather creaked from the sanitation chemicals. Pretending she didn't care what had previously happened in the tan chair or

how many times, she fished up the jack-in cord, sliding it into her port slot at the base of her neck with practiced ease. She saw St. Rachel assume the other chair, while the Orange Lady sat at the screen and keyboard, adjusting the VR cap that sat cockeyed on her head over the elaborate, overly thick coils of her artificial hair.

What kind of idiot was she to put her life in the hands of such questionable people with such questionable motives?

And yet her instincts...

The world and its other problems melted away once she hit the button to jack into the system. Having already preset the destination, she opened her digital eyes to see the stage projected in front of her in an otherwise black empty space without end. She glanced around and noted a few other figures there, but they were simply dark shadows with vague, humanoid forms, each neutral avatar representing a potential bidder at the auction. She wondered how many of them were a single person running multiple accounts or pre-programmed bots. It didn't matter; each account represented competition.

Since it was all for anonymity's sake, St. Augustina couldn't be entirely sure which ones were St. Rachel and the Orange Lady. Glancing up at the stage, the MC was now about halfway down the line of maybe a dozen people. The personal presentation was an attempt to up each lot's value, and if they didn't sell then as a whole of the potentially lucrative lots. And each was a pile of body parts if they didn't sell at all.

In front of each avatar, including St. Augustina, hung a tiny screen. Like the other pages they had looked at earlier, this one was a list, but it was now a little more curated than the others. Each lot had a single well-thought-out title. The Mistress. The Researcher. The Saint. Clicking through brought up an encrypted file with the stats of each. The bidding bar and button were already active inside each lot, with a few early bids inputted. There was also a dialogue box, with a white bar above it that allowed guests an opportunity to ask questions about each lot in real-time. The MC would occasionally pause his spiel to answer them.

That gave her an idea.

In the virtual world, St. Augustina didn't need the visual analog to access her holodesk. She only needed to picture it in her mind or feel it on instinct, since her brain was the interface. Finding her sync to St. Rachel still live, she imported it into the auction's system, opening her own dialogue box, this one with a black bar to indicate that it was in privacy mode.

"St. Rachel, can you hear me?"

"*Yes,*" her temporary partner responded.

"Which one do you think is the Orange Lady?"

"I already have a connection with her," St. Rachel replied. "Give me a moment to import her."

"*She's on a semi-public computer, that's not safe,*" St. Augustina warned, but the other Saint ignored her, and soon, the dialogue box had expanded to include their unwelcome third party.

"*Oh, this is so cool,*" the Orange Lady practically squealed, and St. Augustina was grateful no one else in the digital room could hear their teeny-bopper.

"I'm sending you the sniper program; accept the file you're about to receive. Orange Lady, you don't do anything. I've already imported it into the computer you're using," St. Rachel informed them, her cool business demeanor being the first reassuring thing that had happened on this operation. At least it wasn't a hundred percent amateur hour.

St. Augustina felt the files arrive and installed them with a thought. A new button appeared on her virtual terminal, next to the bid button. It was a matching button with a bull's-eye icon in it.

"When it gets down to the last ten seconds of the auction, all three of us are going to hit the new button, the one that looks like a bull's-eye. There will be others trying to do this, but each press by us will be over a thousand bids at once. Just keep clicking it until I say stop, even if the timer runs out. This should flood the system with our bids, locking out anyone else, so that one of us will be the final bidder."

"*Each of those bids will add more money to the total,*" St. Augustina said, suddenly picturing an astronomical amount that they would never be able to pay.

"Each bid will be one-tenth of a credit. It'll probably add a few hundred, maybe even a thousand, but nothing we can't cover. Come on, St. Augustina. Have more faith in me." St. Augustina had to admit, St. Rachel's program was very impressive. Of course, she couldn't believe she was getting enthusiastic about anything that was going to help St. Benedict. Life certainly liked laughing at her.

There was nothing else left to do but wait for the presentation to be over, so she settled back, figuratively speaking.

The MC was parading around an augmented mistress, and St. Augustina wished she could mute him.

The latest offering wore a cocktail dress with LEDs sewn in that changed the color of the dress as she walked. She was made up as a model, but moved shyly, looking like she was unused to moving that quickly in heels that high. A collar was fitted around her neck, and she was led on a gold chain by the MC, who gave knowing nods and winks to the expressionless, mute avatars.

He went on to read her stats, but St. Augustina wasn't really listening to him. Instead, she focused on the woman, wishing she could let her know that... what? That she wasn't alone? That someone felt sympathy for her? She *was* alone. And what would St. Augustina's sympathy really do to change her circumstance? It wasn't going to stop the woman from being auctioned off to whoever wanted a private sex-slave, or programmed to be the perfect "whatever they wanted." Someone they could abuse however and whenever they wanted, and she would be completely at their mercy. Her augmentations made her into a thing, her body and mind already violated even before that moment. There had been a reason that St. Rachel's augmentations were more stable than St. Augustina's. They were advanced and time-tested. Because whenever in human history, when presented with new technology, had human beings not used it for sex first?

"What is it that disturbs you so much about this?" the Orange Lady asked.

"*It doesn't disturb* you?" St. Augustina challenged.

"It does, but I'm looking at your face right now, and you look like you're in pain."

"*Just never you mind. You wouldn't understand,*" St. Augustina dismissed her, focusing on her body far, far away and telling it to relax.

"You have no way of knowing what I would or wouldn't understand."

"Have you been used as a guinea pig, cut up and violated to become something someone else wanted you to be?"

There was a long pause. "*No.*"

"Then, trust me, you would not understand."

"You want to save her, don't you?" the Orange Lady asked.

"*Leave her alone,*" St. Rachel added.

"*She isn't the mission.*" St. Augustina answered anyway, forcing her virtual eyes to look into the middle distance so she didn't have to register what was happening, didn't have to see the stage, didn't have to acknowledge what she wasn't doing. The Orange Lady's words were getting to her. She needed to hold it together.

"So what? What's stopping you from following your desires?"

"Leave me alone."

"I'm not threatening you, Saint. If you want me to bid on her, I will."

"You can't do that, we have to concentrate our resources on acquiring St. Benedict. We lose him, we lose everything," St. Rachel said. "This is his life we're talking about."

"What do you want to do, St. Augustina?"

St. Augustina blinked, jacking out of the machine, and finally looked back at the Orange Lady with her real eyes, who returned a Cheshire-cat smile. "We have a mission that you hired us to accomplish. Why are you getting in the way?" St. Augustina demanded.

"Because you asked me to and I could," she said sweetly.

"I didn't ask you for anything..."

"Are you sure? You said you wanted your freedom."

This teeny-bopper's ability to render the Saint speechless was getting very annoying.

"I also love helping return lost children home," the Orange Lady said with her own child-like smile.

"She's not a child."

"She is to someone."

"We can't bid on them all. St. Rachel's right, we need to focus on acquiring St. Benedict."

"Then why are you even talking to me about it?" the Orange Lady asked, her eyes reflecting a deeper wisdom that defied her youthful features.

St. Augustina's mouth opened and closed like a fish.

"I think that's the real reason you agreed to help me. That's what you really want to do. You want to help," the Orange Lady said.

St. Augustina couldn't deny the truth in her words. She had heard the turn of phrase "words that cut straight to the heart," but this was the first time she understood what those words meant. It was like she couldn't breathe, the ache went so deep.

"We could save her..." she heard herself say as if unsure what she was saying.

Just then, St. Rachel jacked out as well. Opening her eyes, she leaned forward in her chair, looking very put out. "St. Benedict is next in case you two are done possibly throwing over the entire operation."

St. Augustina leaned back into her chair, not taking her eyes from the Orange Lady. "Then, do it."

The Orange Lady smiled.

"Do what? What the hell are we doing now?" St. Rachel practically shouted.

"The Orange Lady is going to place a bid on the mistress. One click," St. Augustina said, holding up a finger to emphasize it. The Orange Lady nodded.

"And what, pray tell, are we going to do with an augmented mistress?"

"Save her."

"Oh, well, that's nice. How nice of us," St. Rachel slammed back in the chair and jacked back in.

St. Augustina knew she was being stupid and sentimental, but a weight felt like it had lifted off her shoulders as she jacked herself back in too. Maybe that was all she really could expect from life? Moments like this when the weight lifted, just a little bit. Could that be called redemption?

As soon as she was logged back in, St. Rachel popped up into the dialogue box again. "*St. Augustina! It's St. Ben.*"

Looking at the stage, she saw him, torn between a groan and alarm.

He was shirtless.

If the MC had paraded the mistress with flare, this was close to a Magic Mike performance. Strutting down the stage, St. Benedict had his hands laced behind his head. He was wearing his black combat pants, which seemed to emphasize the nakedness of the muscles on his otherwise lean body. For the life of her, she couldn't understand why they let him keep the damn fedora.

"Don't get too excited, ladies and gentlemen," the MC cooed from his mike, stopping St. Benedict's progress via an electronic umbilical cord, instead of a leash, that seemed to be connected to his head. That stopped

St. Augustina's heart cold. "This item may look like a hot piece of flesh, and he's playful too, but there's more under the hat, so to speak. Shall we have him take it all off?"

While the avatars' expressions remained neutral, many of them had been interacting with their lists. Now all of them were looking up, attending the performance in front of them, the first real spark of genuine interest any of them had shown all night. But, then, he had that effect on people, with his smile and charisma.

"Do you want to see?" the MC continued, unnecessarily baiting the silent crowd. He seemed to have noticed that he had the digital room's attention and was enjoying his moment to shine too much. "Oh, and we are getting flooded with questions. Okay, okay, people. We will answer all of them, I promise, but first, let me finish giving you his stats, and let's see if we already have answers for you." Then there was an awkward pause, the MC's eyes staring out, his smile beginning to droop. St. Augustina recognized the winces of pain at the corner of his eyes.

"*What's going on?*" the Orange Lady asked.

"He's getting flooded with questions. I'm not sure how he's receiving them," St. Augustina said.

"I'm going to venture that he has an implant," St. Rachel added.

"*Hmm, maybe.*" St. Augustina would have squinted if she was looking at him with her real eyes. "*Something seems off with St. Benedict, though.*"

"He seems to be having a good time," the Orange Lady commented.

"He's trying to be brave," St. Augustina answered, grimly. "He makes things a game when he's terrified."

"Alright, alright! Time to give the people what they want," the MC said through a clenched smile. He gave the cord an exaggerated tug, which made St. Benedict's own smile stiffen a minute. "I said, give the people what they want."

St. Benedict responded by undulating his body from the toes up, finally snatching the hat off his head, and tossing it out into the crowd. The hat disappeared from sight, but St. Augustina knew it had probably landed in the actual room they were holding him.

Though there was no reaction from the avatars themselves, the shocked looks from the line behind him told the story.

Capped on St. Benedict's head was an electronic monstrosity. It looked like something out of a horror show. The last time St. Augustina remembered seeing something akin to it was during training, shortly after they had first gotten their implants. It was a remote network jack that allowed someone from the outside to control a Saint's implants without their permission. The experience was as painful as it sounded.

The MC was obviously sweating. "Y-yes folks, what you see before you is a much-rumored Saint. These beings are designed with the very latest in technological advancements." The MC gestured at his assistant, who was manipulating something on a tablet. The umbilical came to life, with small blips of light activating along the cord and over the cap. Unable to fight the pain the device created, St. Benedict groaned. His hands automatically went toward the cap, probably to tear it off as his animal brain reacted, while the device detached his thinking mind, taking over. Two guards appeared, grabbing his arms to prevent him from saving himself. Unable to resist the pain, his knees buckled as they forced him to kneel. Not a soul looked away.

"*Oh god,*" St. Rachel whispered, and St. Augustina wished her voice would work to echo it.

Then a holographic icon appeared above his head projected by the headset.

There was a murmur of awe from the other prisoners on the stage, the only human reactions in the room. St. Augustina wondered if they were a good analog for the reactions the avatars must have been having wherever the real people were. Or were they simply as cold and empty of real feeling as the MC and his assistant or the guards?

"Yes, folks, you too can have your own personal one-man army. Espionage, government work, necessary if unlawful activities..." The hologram changed, showing scenes of each thing MC listed being done by other Saints. St. Augustina watched as they hacked into the internal memory recorder all of their brain implants had. It had recorded all the things St. Benedict had seen, playing out his most private memories for all to see, including a brief shot of herself.

She was standing amongst a group of people in a parking lot, dressed in a business suit, holding a gun and a badge. She was flanked by two familiar faces doing the same. When was this? What was she doing?

Somewhere far, far away was a whinny.

"*Stay calm,*" the Orange Lady said. "*Breathe.*" At the command St. Augustina did, her body suddenly remembering how to in a big, gulping rush.

"Truly your imagination is the limit," the MC concluded triumphantly, then gestured at his assistant to stop.

The hologram died on a final image of a familiar woman's face, her eyes glowing white. Was that another Saint? Why did she look familiar? She had actually flashed several times throughout the violated memories. With her sweetheart face and brown hair...

As the image of the woman's face faded, St. Benedict flopped forward, gasping for air while still suspended by his arms.

"Don't worry folks, he'll be back on his feet in a moment," the MC said, with a casual laugh. Hearing the heavily implied command, St. Benedict lifted his head. He swallowed, and for a moment, St. Augustina was sure he was going to throw up. Instead, he leaned and planted a foot on the floor. Moving with more will than strength, he managed to regain both of his feet, the guards doing their part to steady him.

St. Augustina couldn't shake it, the certain feeling that this plan wasn't going to work. She had no logic for it, no obvious reason to think that, yet the feeling had taken a deep hold on her. Things always went wrong. Especially when St. Benedict was involved. Maybe this idea of freedom was a bad illusion? Was it worth going through all of this for a relative concept? Yet, it wouldn't matter, would it? Someone was targeting her. She was involved whether she had a choice or not.

While she was lost in thought, the MC continued with his presentation of the other prisoners. There were only a couple left, and after St. Benedict, most of the room seemed to have lost interest again. She checked his bid screen and saw that a small bidding war had already started. A timer underneath was counted down from an hour. They weren't giving too much time for this online auction, but then, it was an illegal human activity. The longer they went on, the more risk to the whole operation.

She was so tired of thinking about this kind of stuff: calculating what bad people would do and figuring out how to counteract it, especially since much of the time, she wasn't necessarily the good guy either.

"*What do we do now?*" the Orange Lady asked.

"*We wait for the timer to run out,*" St. Rachel said after a moment.

While they waited, St. Augustina flipped over to the augmented mistress's page. She looked like someone, but she couldn't remember who. The woman was of medium height, with a sweetheart face and golden hair that was probably natural because the popular thing to do right now was to dye hair unnatural colors. In many ways, they were nothing alike. Except maybe the look. Even in her thumbnail picture in the file, the mistress looked frightened and tired and too young to have all of her choices taken away.

Reading through her file, going over the small number of details of the woman's life, St. Augustina ticked the small box with a caption beside that said, "Watch this bid." When she returned to St. Benedict's page, a small banner appeared at the bottom of the list with the woman's thumbnail and a "place a bid" bubble automatically set for one credit as well as St. Rachel's sniper button.

"Remember to click the mistress's button at five seconds," St. Augustina said.

"St. Benedict is our priority," St. Rachel reminded them all. "We start clicking at ten seconds. We have no other idea how many other bots we're fighting with, so every click counts."

St. Augustina's stomach tightened as the clock continued to run down. Far away, she could feel her body's anxiety flooding into her virtual self. It wouldn't be her finger or even her virtual finger pressing the button, but her mind imagining it so. The clock was down to fifteen seconds. Then ten.

"*Go!*" St. Rachel said, and she was off. Clicking the button for all it was worth.

St. Augustina saw her avatar's randomly generated name, then another name, then St. Rachel's avatar name all competing for the bid in a flash of nanoseconds.

Five seconds left.

"*We're losing the mistress!*" the Orange Lady said.

No!

St. Augustina glanced down at the bar. There had only been one shot, and it hadn't worked.

"*Don't!*" was all St. Rachel got out.

Three seconds.

St. Augustina started clicking the mistress's button.

Two.

One.

Then the bidding shut down. The virtual screens locked.

Trying to gather her wits, St. Augustina stared down at the screen, trying to make sense of the words now covering the boxes. It had all happened too fast.

"Winner!" was covering the thumbnail face of the mistress.

"Sorry!" was covering St. Benedict's.

"St. Rachel, did you win him?" There was nothing. "Orange Lady. St. Rachel!"

"No. No, I didn't get him. I'm sorry," the Orange Lady said.

"*I got him,*" St. Rachel said, and relief turned St. Augustina's limbs to water.

They had done it. It was almost anti-climactic.

"What's happening?" St. Rachel abruptly said. "What was that? Did you feel..."

And then she was gone.

A cold-hot painful sensation tore through St. Augustina's perception, like she was being ripped backward through an ice bath, then into a lava flow. She knew what was happening, some calm part of her mind comprehended it. She was being forcibly jacked out.

At first, St. Augustina couldn't blink her eyes; the world around her was bleary and out of focus. Two dark shapes stared down at her, manipulating her gummy-like body. She didn't have control back yet, her mind temporarily still separated from her body, even as her awareness returned first. A side effect of being Dorothy-ed like that. Any moment, she would be able to blink and fight, but by then it might be too late to do any good. Her wrists were already bound together.

Standing over her, the two neo-ninjas cemented into reality, their black-masked faces with their bug-like eye covers eliciting an involuntary screech from St. Augustina's dry throat. Across the room, two more hauled St. Rachel out of her chair. Her feet and hands were already bound and her mouth gagged, but it didn't stop her from bucking against the zip ties they had used

to bind her. Throwing her weight around was making it difficult for them, and one ended up dropping her feet.

St. Augustina's feet weren't bound yet.

The two neo-ninjas above her used their weight to hold her down while two others grasped at her legs to allow the fifth to bind them together. They did not expect her to be able to fight back, which resulted in the fifth one getting cracked in the face with her foot. The one holding her right leg was levered off the ground as if riding a steel piston and did not recover their feet well. St. Augustina rotated her hips to the left and pushed back the one holding her left leg, then rocked the other way, attempting to upset herself out of the chair. Her attackers all shouted in alarm, trying to hold and pile on.

She arched the other way and managed a kick across her body into the original unsteady man, knocking him back even further. It was an impossible feat of strength that helped to finally get St. Augustina the momentum she needed to tip out of the chair onto her feet. The move pulled her from the grips of the panicked neo-ninjas, all of this happening very fast even for them.

Pushing off from the floor like a frog, St. Augustina barreled her head into the side of the closest standing ninja. As he hit the wall behind him, she felt cracking bone as the ribs in his side shattered.

She wasted no time, recoiling onto her feet to spin around, her augmented eyes flaring to life with a triple blink. The Orange Lady was being held against another wall by her own two neo-ninjas, one of them shouting orders at the others to restrain the free Saint. She went for the Orange Lady's captors first.

Torn between holding their captive and deflecting her oncoming attack, the closest one reacted too slowly. St. Augustina brought down her bound arms across his face, twisting his neck too far and knocking him out cold. While he spun and dropped away, the other, smarter neo-ninja brought out a knife to set to the Orange Lady's throat before he pulled her between himself and St. Augustina.

What he didn't count on was the Orange Lady disappearing while in his grasp. One second she was there, looking very frightened, and the next, she dissipated into a cloud of woman-shaped sparkles. St. Augustina didn't let her surprise stop her from sending a kick into the guy's chest. He flew backward and slammed hard against the wall, crumpling to the ground like he had been hit by a car. For all intents and purposes, he had. His knife dropped toward the ground, and with a smooth kneeling motion, she caught it in midair.

Now she was armed.

Her augmented sight showed her a path out. Overlaying a flashing escape route on her vision, a small countdown timer appeared in the corner of her vision. Three seconds remained until the opportunity was gone. St. Rachel was near the door, but her bucking had caused her captors to drop her. Rolling into exposed legs, St. Rachel knocked over two of the neo-ninjas focused on St. Augustina. It didn't take them out, but it did distract them enough to increase the probability of escape. St. Augustina simply had to run for it and abandon her partner.

She took it.

Moving faster than a normal person, she stepped and dodged around the jack-in chairs before stepping into a spin to bring the knife blade across an opponent who was moving in fast to intercept her. She wasn't sure what part of him she hit, but blood hit her warm in the face. Unfortunately, his move set her off course, and she tripped over St. Rachel.

Arms came down above her, and she lashed out with the knife again, scoring another hit, but knocking the blade away from her slipping grip. She thrashed, and her augmented strength won her another unfair hit, beating out his heightened ability to dodge, knocking him away from her.

She began to roll again toward the door, bringing her knees around to leverage herself to her feet. In a moment of chaotic synchronicity, it put St. Rachel's bound feet in front of her as well as the knife spinning on the floor. It took two seconds to recover the knife and slice it through the tough plastic band holding her temporary partner's feet. There was a second band at her knees, but cutting through that would cost her time.

"Run, you idiot!" St. Rachel shouted, having managed to spit the gag out of her mouth enough to form words. "Stop being noble and leave me!"

Somehow, hearing St. Rachel say that resolved St. Augustina's mind to continue to do the opposite.

The knife was through the plastic band at St. Rachel's legs just in time for someone to punch St. Augustina across the face. Her vision went starry. Then black. She could still hear shouts around her, hollowly.

Oh crap. She missed the opportunity to escape.

Her augmented vision kept functioning, though, and she punched at an outline of a figure. It was pretty weak, and her thinking brain couldn't communicate to her arms to remind them that they were still bound. She had enough time to think, *I should have used the knife to cut my own ties first*, and about the instructions stewardesses give on airplanes about putting your own mask on first before helping others. Then even the augmented vision disintegrated into blackness. Maybe it was better that way.

Off in the distance, a whinny sounded.

"I know, I know," she muttered. "I am yours. Now dream."

CHAPTER 8

The woman sat in the diner, overlooking the city beyond. The diner was empty. Not a soul to be found.

It was strange, actually. She had been sitting there for a while, waiting for her client, but no one had come in. At this time of night, the diner should have been busy, people waking up and looking for their first meal of the day. Half the neon in the room was off. Only the section she was sitting in had any glow, which was especially odd since it should have been all one continual circuit. The auto-waitress was the only thing moving, coming around a few times to refill her synth-coffee, but even that pre-programmed machine hadn't said two words to her.

It refilled her cup again, and she sighed before reaching for the bowl of individually packaged creamers to see if they had any hazelnut. That was when she noticed the chained manacles around her wrists. She had been wearing them the whole time, but it was like she was only just then noticing. There was about a foot of chain between her wrists and a connected chain that linked to a bolted panel in the middle of the table. Staring at it, she wondered how long it had been there. Then on her periphery, she saw a second synth-coffee cup being lifted up.

Sitting back, she blinked as she looked across the table to see St. Benedict, also chained to the table and drinking synth-coffee.

He was staring out the window like she had been, dressed with his stupid fedora. His black army-cut shirt was a relief to her eyes versus the last time she had seen him, which was…

She double-blinked. Why couldn't she remember? She felt like she had seen him recently, and she had been doing something concerning him, but it dissipated from her mind like a dream upon waking. She was pretty sure it involved him not wearing a shirt. He was definitely wearing a black, long-sleeved shirt now, reinforcement patches over each shoulder.

As if feeling her eyes on him, he turned to look at her.

"Oh! You see me now?"

She furrowed her eyebrows at him. "What the hell does that mean?"

He smiled and held out his cup to the auto-waitress, who refilled it. "I keep asking this thing for pie, but it only brings more synth-coffee."

"St. Benedict," St. Augustina said, with lots of warning in her voice. She had no patience for his bullshit.

She heard the whinny again, this time louder and close by. Jumping in her skin, she turned to look out the window. Dark swirling fog blotted out the lights of the city as a red-eyed unicorn monster paced past the window. It stared at her angrily through the glass. St. Augustina tried to stand up to put distance between them, but the chain prevented it. Still, she maintained the strained distance as the creature continued to slowly walk past, moving along the windows, then past the door for a heart-wrenching second.

"He's been doing that for a while. Don't worry. He can't get in," St. Benedict said, calmly sipping his synth-coffee.

"Why the hell not?"

"Don't know exactly, been trying to figure it out. There's nothing else to do," he said.

"St. Benedict." St. Augustina slapped the table with her hand. "Answer me. What are you doing here? Where are we?"

He heaved a big sigh, stirring his synth-coffee with a thin, plastic straw. "Look, St. Auggie, I'm not trying to be obtuse here. It's just that… that is probably the dozenth time you've asked me the same series of questions in…" he looked out the window, "I'm not sure how long we've been here; there is no sense of time in this place. But believe me, you've already asked me that, and I've explained what's happening a few different ways. Then after a while, you seem to forget again. You even forget I'm sitting here."

He took a long, noisy drink of his synth-coffee, looking at her over the rim. "So, if it's all the same to you, can we talk about something else for a while until you forget again?"

St. Augustina stared at him, processing what he was telling her. "How many different answers have you given me?"

He chuffed a dry, sour laugh. "Okay, I guess that's a new question." He set down his cup, then brought the little bowl of creamers to himself and started building a little fort with them. "I think I've told you the whole truth once, various lies previously. Some outlandish. You were not amused. Don't know what psycho crap is happening to you, but we seem to be safest where we are right now."

"Safest?"

"At one point, you seemed to remember everything, and then we were sitting in a graveyard without these nice walls to keep him away," St. Benedict said, nodding at the black unicorn. This time when it passed, it swiped with a leonine paw at the window, its talons scraping painfully against the glass.

"What the hell?!" St. Augustina said, jumping backward again, only to be stopped by the chain. "What is wrong with that thing?"

"Eh, it's getting testy, I guess."

"What's wrong with its feet!?"

"What, the paws?"

"It's a unicorn with paws!"

"It's a Poh, some sort of really awful unicorn monster that eats people. They come from a region in northern China or something. But actually... now, this is a fun fact I haven't told you yet, that is not actually a Poh either." He leaned his elbow as far as his chain would let him, on top of the back of the booth, to twist toward the Poh as it continued its prowl. "That is actually a piece of the Oberon." He waggled his eyebrows at her with a nod as if to say, *Isn't that cool?*

"The Oberon?" St. Augustina asked. "As in... the Faerie King?"

"Yeah," St. Benedict said, nodding as he turned back to mess with his creamer fort some more, changing it from a fort to a tower. "Had one of those nasty buggers in my psyche before as well. Only reason I think I was able to identify what was going on with you."

"This is so weird. Why do I know who the Oberon is?" St. Augustina asked, leaning her head forward onto her palms. She did. She knew exactly who St. Benedict was referring to. The Faerie King. Something about that helped calm her. Maybe this was what happened when one finally snapped?

"Don't worry. You'll forget again soon," St. Benedict said, nonplussed.

The auto-waitress appeared once more with its synth-coffee pot. "CAN I GET YOU ANYTHING?"

St. Benedict paused in the construction of his tower to look at the auto-waitress. "Okay," he said warily, "that's the first time it's done that."

"Can we have some pie, please?" St. Augustina asked.

"WHAT FLAVOR?"

"St. Ben?" she asked.

"Uh, I'll have whatever berry you've got," he said.

"A LA MODE?" the auto-waitress asked.

"Yeah, thank you," St. Benedict agreed, then he darted a look at St. Augustina.

She nodded thoughtfully. "I'll have a Dutch apple." He raised his eyebrows in surprise, and she shrugged back. "What diner doesn't have a Dutch apple? I want ice cream too."

"BE RIGHT BACK," the auto-waitress said, and it zipped away to the silent kitchen.

"I wonder if it's really coming back with pie?"

"Okay, St. Ben... What?" she asked as he turned back at her to give her a too-pleased smile. "Why are you looking at me like that?"

"You do know that is the first time you've ever called me St. Ben?"

"No, it's the third time," she said, with mock admonishment.

"When were the other times?"

"Just now was the second."

"And the first?"

She studied his face a moment, watching him think. Then, as he remembered. "Oh, yes. You're right. That night."

She nodded with him, feeling weary. "Yeah, that night."

The diner vanished around them, and they were there in that joint cell. They were both still chained, but they sat next to each other on the floor. Her head was on his lap, and he was stroking her hair, gently threading his fingers through her tight curls. The Deacons had chopped her hair extremely short, and it was only starting to grow back at that point. There was blood crusted in it, and he was carefully working it out as he stroked.

"This was the night I almost gave up," she said softly, not at all surprised at the change of the world around them. She was ready to go wherever this craziness led.

"Yeah," he said heavily. She knew his face was as roughed up as hers. His hair was also shorn close to his head, the puckering scar along his cranium clearly visible. She realized lying there, picturing it, the scar was why he always wore hats whenever he could, even if you couldn't see it through his hair.

"You said we've been jumping from place to place when we're not in the diner. Have we been here yet?" she asked, studying the hair-thin crack across the small room. She had studied every inch of this cell while waiting for the next training phase or the next experiment.

"No. No, we haven't." His voice was gruff and hoarse. He had been shouting so much that day he had strained it, trying to save St. Cornelius.

"What is going on?" she whispered to the wall. "Why can we magically transport from one memory to another?" She let the question resonate within her. "It's not magic, is it? We're inside my head."

"Yes," he said tiredly.

"That means you aren't really St. Benedict, are you? You're really my memory of St. Benedict."

"No, I am really St. Benedict. Like I said before, Lady Ursula contacted us, or rather she contacted me to ask for my help in getting through to you."

"And who is Lady Ursula?" St. Augustina asked, turning her face to look up. "What does she want with me?"

A ghost of a smile whispered across his face. "You know her as the Orange Lady. As to what she wants with you... I actually don't know. I coerced St. Rachel after the first time you jailed my consciousness inside your labyrinth here. Remotely, of course. I pretty much was only able to send her a message using your software when you were rebooting again. Predictable as clockwork, she answered Lady Ursula's call instead of her MO of ignoring it. Then she showed up and dove in to save me. Now we seem to be in a repetitive loop in your head, while whatever the Poh is trying to do is keeping you out of Lady Ursula's power."

"So, this place is a nice change of pace?" she asked, her voice cracking even as she sounded amused. The weariness felt bone deep. She didn't know if she could lift her head again. How long had this nightmare been going on?

"Yeah, thank you. It's great to be back here in this jail cell. Never mind the bazillion trips down memory lane that I've worked so hard to deny."

"Like what else?" St. Augustina asked, turning her face back toward the wall.

"Bolivia."

St. Augustina made a disgusted noise in her throat. "Okay, that's plenty. Don't tell me anymore."

Silence overcame them both, and St. Augustina focused on his fingers in her hair. It still felt so good.

"St. Ben, what is going on here? Why is this happening?" Her voice sounded small, even to her. Really it was barely a whisper, which was more than enough to hear within the dismally silent prison.

"Then or now?" he asked, matching her tone.

She sighed hard. "Both, I guess."

"Sorry, old habits." He sighed as well. "What is happening now is we think your brain is defending itself against the magic that has invaded your being. It's eating you up from the inside."

That took a moment to process. "Magic is real?"

"Yes. Honestly, we've talked about this a half-dozen times already. It's absolutely fascinating that you created a world in your mind where magic simply doesn't exist. I can't even imagine all the implications of that."

She sat up to look at him. He blinked, almost blushing at how close they were. She realized he must have thought she was going to kiss him, considering the proximity.

"Why did they put you in my cell back then? It wasn't normal practice."

"I think at the time, they expected me to fuck you back to life."

She dryly chuckled, looking down shyly. "Well, damn it, this is awkward."

He joined in the laugh. "They didn't say it directly. And, well, come on, it wasn't that absurd. Human comfort was something we were starving for."

"I mean it'd be like kissing my brother or cousin or something," she said, her mouth smiling and twisting in disgust at the same time.

"I know what you mean," St. Benedict thankfully agreed. "That wasn't how it was between us, but the Deacons didn't understand that. For all their knowledge and statistics and mastery of manipulation, they forgot one fundamental fact."

"They were human too," she said, nodding.

"Yeah, they were susceptible to statistics just as much as we were. Susceptible to human nature and human desires and human blindness. That's something that people in power always seem to forget. Humanity. It's not like you can just shrug it off and it goes away because you think you're a god now. I knew what they expected of us, and for every time they were right, they were wrong."

"Why didn't you let me die that night?"

St. Benedict covered his face. "This is why we came here, isn't it? This is why your psyche can't move on from this cycle of dreams."

"I've hated you for years based on what I thought the answer was. I don't want to hate you anymore, St. Benedict, but you are going to have to give me a good damn reason."

Outside the cell came a screaming whinny followed by a hard thump on the metal door to their cell. St. Augustina ignored it. She was starting to understand what was happening, why she was here at all. "If my brain is fighting to defend itself, you're here to help me navigate my way out, but you still haven't given me the final key. That's why it had to be you. I would never come back here by myself."

The cell disappeared again. They were back in the diner, facing each other, this time with a piece of pie each.

"Why did you promise me that we were in this together and then leave me to die as soon as it suited you?"

"It wasn't..." but St. Benedict stopped. He shoved his pie away, thrusting his head in his hands.

"Wasn't like that? Is that what you were going to say?" St. Augustina finished for him.

"Yes, I was going to say exactly that," St. Benedict owned, before dropping his head onto the table, knocking his hat askew. "Look, I know how it sounds, but at the moment when I told you that it *was* you and me against the world, I did mean it. I wasn't lying to you at the time I said it. I turned it into a lie later." He sat back, facing her like a man washed out by a current that wouldn't stop running over him.

"Just tell me why," she pressed.

He continued to struggle.

"St. Benedict!"

"That's not my name, okay?! Stop calling me that."

She jutted out her jaw at that. "And what was *my* name?"

"Idrina. You told me that night."

"Yes, I did. Idrina, you said, you can't give up. You can't quit. You asked me if I had anybody out there waiting for me, anyone who might be looking for me. I told you about my mother. My mother! What she meant to me, what I last said to her. I told her that I hated her, the last fucking thing I said to her before I escaped like a stupid child, and she was right. I shouldn't have gone to that party. I should have stayed home, where I was safe, but I didn't listen, did I? I wanted to be my own person, and somehow, walking away from her was going to prove that."

"Idrina..."

"And you told me it was all right. That it wasn't my fault."

St. Benedict ran his fingers violently through his hair, knocking his fedora back. "What did I say wasn't your fault?"

"Don't get exasperated with me!" St. Augustina snapped back.

"Idrina!"

The familiar voice snapped St. Augustina's resurfacing rage into icy stillness. She looked toward where the diner's kitchen should have been and instead saw her mother's front room. Standing in front of the couch, with her fists planted on her hips, her mother was staring her down. She was older than in the picture in front of the helicopter. Still fit, still on active duty, but preparing to retire soon.

Young Idrina appeared in front of her, dressed in her Foxy Brown costume. Her arms were crossed, and her hips were jutted out to the side so far she looked like she could fold up into an accordion. The whole time her lip was thrust forward in an annoyed sneer.

"Idrina! Are you listening to me?" her mother demanded.

"What do you know!?" Idrina shouted, straightening up suddenly. Her voice broke into a squeak as she continued to shout. "It's not like you've been around! It's not like you raised me or anything. What the hell do you know?"

The barb hit her tough mother exactly where she wanted, tears appearing in the corners of her mother's eyes, even as they flared to a new height of anger.

"You ungrateful, self-centered, little bitch!" Her mother's hand flew, hitting her across the face, doing what it was meant to, shock the hell out of her. Yet, her teenage mind filed it away as more evidence, more proof that her mother was the bad guy, unjust, and amoral. Especially after her much stronger mother marched her by the arm to her room and slammed the door. "You will stay here until I tell you to come out, do you hear me!?" she ordered through the door, muffling her voice only a little.

"*You're* the bitch," the teenager muttered, sitting on her bed for only a moment, before heading over to her window and the fire escape her mother conveniently forgot. She stared at the window, her hand hesitating on the latch, not at all feeling comfortable with the decision to rebel.

"If I had just stayed there like she told me to. Acted with honor..."

"Fuck you," the teenage Idrina said out loud and unlatched the window and went out. The memory faded into an impression of the diner again, which didn't fully form before it began to change again.

"You think your mama is proud of you now, bitch?" a gruff voice laughed from nowhere.

"Of course she's not looking for you. She probably just thought you ran away and decided not to come home," a woman's sour voice echoed.

"Do you think she'd want you home now, after all that you've done?" her own voice argued angrily.

"It wasn't your fault," St. Benedict's voice cut through.

They were back in the cell, though this time, the Saints still sat at the diner table. Instead of being in the memory, they were looking toward where the kitchen should have been, looking down on themselves sitting against the prison cell wall. It was surreal and yet correct, according to the rules of dreams.

"What do you mean? Of course, it was my fault," the St. Augustina from the past said bitterly.

"You and your mom had a fight. Teenagers and parents do that. That shit's normal," St. Benedict said. "There was no way you could have known this would happen to you."

"My mother knew."

"No, she didn't. She worried something like this could happen, but exactly that? People don't get kidnapped off the streets to be turned into living bio-weapons. It's just not a thing people worry about."

"It's my fault..."

"It's *their* fault. No one made them do this to us; they don't have a divine right to it. You made a teenage mistake, and you know what," he looked at her sideways, "just forgive yourself for it already. I can guarantee your mother already has if she remembers it at all."

Tears streamed down the past St. Augustina's face. Whatever little bit of control her self-contempt had reined in was gone. She collapsed sideways at the lightest touch of St. Benedict's hand, her head landing in his lap.

"Out of all of us here, you're the real innocent," he said.

The memory faded into blackness, leaving the current St. Augustina glaring at the current St. Benedict, who struggled to meet her eyes.

"How could you?" Tears streamed down her face, burning trails as hot as lava.

"I don't see how what I did was a bad thing here," he said, his voice sounding weak.

"You made me believe in you. You do that, don't you," she said softly, turning her gaze down at her pie. "You make people believe in you, have faith, until you need to use them. You manipulated my pain and used the memory of my mother against me. And I'm supposed to forgive you for that?"

She wanted to scream, to be angry, but it was burning away. All she really wanted to do was eat the piece of pie in front of her and forget. Maybe if she walked outside and let the Poh take her again, erase her memory one more time and keep this farce of a nightmare going, she could be content with that.

"Do you remember when I told you about my wife?"

She furrowed her eyebrows. What was he talking about? Looking up at him, St. Augustina tried to recall what he had said.

He didn't wait for her to confirm. "That night... no... even before that... I thought you were just like her. You were the only true innocent amongst us, like I said. Everyone else deserved to be there, but once I understood that you were just taken off the street... You were exactly like her. You didn't deserve what was happening to you at all. I wanted to protect you like I should have her."

"You didn't."

"No, I didn't. When it came down to it, when it was a question of your survival or mine... it felt like a choice between you and her."

"Your wife."

"Yes. I knew in my heart she was out there somewhere. I knew I needed to survive, to make sure she got out all right, that she was all right, after everything I had done to endanger her. I needed her to *be* all right. I needed her to be the beacon of life that got me out of that place. And I started substituting you for her because you were so much like her."

The Poh passed by again, but neither of them noticed. St. Augustina felt like her ears were ringing. What was he saying?

"When the moment came... my first thought was to go out and do a grand last stand, so you could get away. But I knew I would die. And I would fail her. Again. And I realized at that moment that if I chose you over her... Over my own survival... I exist only for her sake..."

"So, you shoved me out the door," St. Augustina said.

"I thought I was sending you to your death."

"Instead, I survived."

He nodded, smiling a ghost of a smile. "Yeah, you did. The Deacons didn't know what to think after that. They were torn about it for weeks after. Had I made the right move or not. Surviving whatever the cost... sacrificing a debatably valuable asset. Was I right, or was I wrong? Because you survived anyway, so you were obviously more valuable to them than originally estimated. You didn't crumple up and die like they thought you would. Instead of breaking into a thousand pieces, you fell and became a knife. That was something they couldn't predict. They wondered if I knew that was what was going to happen; was that why I was so confident in sacrificing you, because I knew you would survive, anyway. It threw off their calculations for months. I don't think they ever pinned it down. Goddamn idiots."

"They didn't see you die inside," St. Augustina said, seeing everything with detached clarity. "You were sacrificing her all over again."

He stared at the table, unresponsive, in a hell of his own making.

"Did you ever find her?" she asked, feeling strangely serene about it all.

"I guess I owe you that much. Yeah. Yeah, I found out what happened to her," he continued to stare at the table, his face both haunted and intense. She could see his suffering and recognize it as her own.

"I wanted to kill you, you know. That was what kept me going, to survive that night. I thought..." she looked out the window, the city glowing beyond. The fake city. The city of her dreams. "I thought, I'll prove him wrong. I defined myself by it. Being the opposite of everything I thought you were." She laughed hollowly to herself. "I failed entirely."

"St. Augustina, please don't do that. You've always been a better person, a better Saint, than I could ever be. You were everything they were looking for..."

"I wanted to be my mother," she said, cutting him off. "Do you understand? That's what they took from me. I wanted to be what she was, and I always felt I could never live up to her, what she was, so I defined myself in opposition to what she was. And then there was you. I defined myself in opposition to what you were."

"Who are you now?" a new voice cut in.

They turned together, staring at the woman who had appeared at the end of their table. She was older, much older, yet majestic in her bearing. Like a queen.

"May I sit?" she asked St. Augustina, inclining her head to her respectfully.

"Yeah, sure," St. Augustina said, then looked at St. Benedict. "I think you can go now. We've covered everything we need to." Reaching out a hand, St. Augustina released St. Benedict from his chains with a touch of her finger. They dropped away instantly, and he rubbed his wrists.

"But, Idrina..." he started, but she raised a chained hand to him.

"Thank you for coming. But you can jack out now. Have St. Rachel run a diagnostic on you, make sure I haven't hurt you. I imagine you've been online and jacked into my brain for a few days now," St. Augustina said. He had the good grace to look sheepish, before nodding, accepting her orders. After that, he dissipated into a shower of light, jacking out of her mind now that she had finally freed him.

Once he was gone, St. Augustina turned to the woman waiting patiently at the end of her table. "I think you should sit down. You probably have the other half of the answers I need."

The woman smiled and slid into the seat St. Benedict had just vacated. She was dressed beautifully, with soft yellow and orange patterns wrapped around her body.

"You are the Orange Lady then?" St. Augustina asked, noting the young woman's face inside the older woman's elegance.

"Yes, though I wasn't thinking when I chose the name. As silly as it sounds, I was wearing orange that day, and then once I had already chosen it as my... avatar, I think is what it's called, it was a bit too late to change it again. We were already burning through too many dream stones before I brought St. Benedict in to help. It was easier to continue under the identity of the Orange Lady since you had at least accepted that identity into your consciousness."

"Why are you trying to help me at all?" St. Augustina asked. "Who are you to me?"

"Honestly, no one. I've never met you before you were brought to me. My understanding was that you had been wandering the streets, mad, talking to yourself, sometimes attacking anyone who crossed your path. As far as I know, no one was seriously hurt, but if someone hadn't recognized the signs of wild curse magic and brought you to me, who knows what might have happened. After seeing inside your dreams, I'm not surprised. It is a dark world you inhabit."

Everything the woman was saying sounded true. Pieces of memory floated up to St. Augustina, confirming her being on the street, flashing on a series of cognizant realities before plunging her back into the sea of madness.

"I was lost in a magical mist with a monster in it," she said, the only understanding she had from that time.

"Yes. The Oberon's curse. The miasma of it penetrated deep into your psyche and drove you mad. Most people it would have outright killed. You are both strong-willed and lucky. The creature possessing you fed off your dreams, which in turn kept you compliant as it ate away at your life force. Normally, a possession like that would have been simple for me to cure, except..."

"I'm not a simple person."

The older woman nodded. "Your augmentations proved to be a problem. They seemed to interact with the magic making my attempts to remove the curse ineffectual."

"The cookie jar," St. Augustina said, putting that piece together. She waved her hand, and her holodesk appeared with the cookie jar smack in the middle. Another lock had undone itself, leaving two more binding the jar together. She lifted it off her holodesk carefully, before dismissing it and setting the jar on the table.

"Yes, this cookie jar," the woman said, nodding at it. "I have yet to understand its importance, but it seems to be the key to all of this."

"It's my black box: a program installed to protect my brain from being hacked. It's all theoretical, but because of the augmentations, it would be possible to hack a consciousness like a computer, making the Saints susceptible to attack. That's why the locks were designed for me to unlock. They were constructed out of my memories."

"When you say constructed...?"

"That cap we saw St. Benedict wearing at the auction. Yes, that is a real thing."

The old woman nodded tersely at that, thinking a moment. "I see. What St. Benedict said makes sense now. He mentioned another way to access your mind but thought the process ran too great a chance of killing you in this state. The human part of you was naturally susceptible to the Poh's magic, but the technological part of you was fighting it, trying to keep you alive..."

"Yes, I think that's right. If we open up this jar, I should be able to reboot the system. And the key is inside," St. Augustina said, examining the two remaining locks. Outside their window, the Poh roared, slamming its horn into the glass, which impossibly repelled it. Both women eyed the creature warily.

"It's only a matter of time before it gets through. Magic degrades technology," St. Augustina said. "My guess is that this diner program is what's left of my firewall, metaphorically speaking." It thrusted again and this time the glass yielded the tiniest crack.

"It senses what you are trying to do," the woman said. "It knows that if you manage to wake up, it will never hold you again."

"How are you so sure of what it knows?" St. Augustina asked, not removing her eyes from the third thrust. The crack in the glass grew wider, its red eyes sharper.

"I am the head of the Inner Council of the Magic Guild," the older woman said before putting her hand out to St. Augustina. "Lady Ursula, by the way. Hopefully, you will remember me this time."

St. Augustina shook the hand a couple of pumps then turned her attention back to the Poh. "Me too. We're running out of time here." The Poh's horn broke through the glass, sliding and screeching along the shaft, setting St. Augustina's teeth on edge.

"You need to open the jar," Lady Ursula said, giving the jar a small push toward St. Augustina.

"I can't!" she responded, starting to lose herself to panic. "There are two more locks to undo."

Then Lady Ursula shifted her gaze away, staring into nothingness. "I'm not sure I have this correct, but I think... St. Benedict is saying..."

"What?"

"He's asking if you'd like help with the last two locks or help with life?" Lady Ursula asked, looking unsure.

"God, that sounds like him. What?!" St. Augustina shouted out loud. "Just tell us what you want to say, you asshole!"

The horn penetrated again, and St. Augustina leaned back to duck underneath it as the glass slowed it enough to keep her from being skewered. The damn creature was breaking through. If it had been real glass, it would have shattered. Apparently, her mind made a diner with shatter-resistant glass.

"St. Benedict!" St. Augustina shouted.

"He says the locks are right next to each other," Lady Ursula said, scuttling out of the booth and away from the horn as the third hole the Poh made broke on her side. Pulling his horn back, he united the first hole with the other two to create a larger one. Sensing his progress, the Poh stopped stabbing and instead flung its entire body weight against the glass, spraying them both with some of the shards. The Poh was almost through.

And she was *still* chained to the table.

St. Augustina pulled the cookie jar toward herself, staring at the locks while she was practically lying on her back. Then she saw what he was referring to. The last two locks were right next to each other, which in some respects, created a hinge. Flipping up the other metal plates that had been held down by the locks, she pulled hard on the lid and it hinged open wide enough for whatever was inside to slide into her hand. She tried not to feel stupid.

The world around her became quiet, even though some part of her noted the flying glass as the Poh breached her defenses. This was it, down to the wire. In the distance, someone screamed her name, but it was mostly hollow and muted. There was pain as claws dug into her body, but none of it mattered.

It wasn't real.

It was only a dream.

In her hands was her Saint Box, carved silver with runes covering each side of it, about the length and depth of her thumb. There was a tiny, articulate pair of hinges and a small tab that held it closed. Blood sprayed behind it. Her mind knew her dream body was being mauled, but strangely she felt no pain. She refused to acknowledge it while it was happening.

It was only a dream, so she didn't feel it anymore.

Instead, she opened the little box. Only *she* could. The world went silent and still as she stared at her mother's dog tags, the pressed metal with scarred, black rubber silencers. Her most precious possession. The thing she valued most was contained within the box.

She had been wearing them that night, the night she had been abducted. Automatically, her mind played the memory out around her. The diner fell away, and she was inside the white van, lying, or rather, being pressed into the cold, humming metal as the vehicle tore away down the street. She felt the men pressing down on her, their laughter. Their awful, cold, bitter laughter as they molested her, putting fingers and tongues where they had no permission to be. Tearing at her sexy costume. Her young body no longer under her control.

Still, she stared into the box. Despite the violence being done to her in the diner, it did not disturb her ability to look inside her Saint Box. More proof that it was all just a dream. Gently, she scooped the dog tags out and ran her fingers over the impressed letters and numbers. Along her mother's name, she traced one finger.

"I'm so sorry, Mom. I'm so, so very sorry."

"St. Augustina," a voice called to her. Not her mother's but still the voice of an older woman, someone she was coming to trust. The nightmare memory was falling away. She felt herself waking up. The Poh was screaming, but she could now tell she didn't hear it with her physical ears.

And then she opened her eyes.

"St. Augustina?" Lady Ursula asked, her eyebrows pinched in worry. She was sitting in front of St. Augustina, her gold eyes studying the Saint's face for some sign of life.

Shaking her head a little, St. Augustina brought her hands to her face and rubbed dry crust from her eyes. "Am I awake?"

The older woman's face broke into a joyful smile, before she wrapped her arms around the younger woman, hugging her too hard. "Yes, child. Yes, you are. At last!"

Dropping her hands, St. Augustina looked slowly about her. They sat in a darkened room with candles all around. The floor was carved in a circle with runes and more candles at different points. Outside the circle, crouched at the edge, was St. Benedict.

He looked pale and sickly; his fedora pushed up high on his head, revealing the peak of his hair. There was also a strange apparatus sliding down his nose, like a pair of sunglasses with a couple of wires coming out of them. The wires snaked through the candles, disappearing behind her, and St. Augustina was sure without looking, they were connected to her. His usually immaculate clothes were sweat-stained and streaked, with the top button of his shirt open. But he smiled a satisfied smile, the corners of his eyes crinkling in a surprising first sign of age that most people showed in their thirties. How much time had really passed since she saw him smile, ages already?

St. Rachel, standing behind him, wasn't smiling. She only looked tired, her arms crossed under her chest as if she was trying to get warm and couldn't, despite the dark sweater she wore that went to her mid-thighs.

"We did it, St. Augustina," St. Benedict said, dropping back to sit on the floor as if he had just finished running a marathon. "We saved you."

Gently, St. Augustina shook her head. "Oh, you idiots," St. Augustina said, her voice cracking as if it hadn't been used for ages. "What have you done?"

CHAPTER 9

"What do you mean, 'idiots?'" St. Benedict said, his smile dropping in confusion.

"We've saved you," St. Rachel said softly with the same confusion.

"No, you haven't." St. Augustina set a hand to her temples, her head throbbing as all her memories came rushing back.

She was complete again.

She was screwed.

"Why couldn't you all leave well enough alone? Why did you wake me up?"

Her three rescuers exchanged glances with each other.

She knew they didn't understand. She supposed it wouldn't make any sense to her either. "Look, I appreciate what you intended to do, but I was where I wanted to be. It was part of my deal... with the creature, the Poh, I guess, and now you've broken it!"

"You wanted to be possessed by the Poh?" St. Rachel asked, her face twisted in disgust. "Why?"

"I had to survive!" St. Augustina stated. She gestured at St. Benedict. "You left me to die..." She stopped. No, that wasn't quite right. She had told him to leave her there. "When I turned down your offer to escape with you from that hell-forsaken place..."

That was when she noticed the fourth person in the room. His was another familiar face, standing just behind St. Rachel, one who filled St. Augustina with contempt.

"You," she nearly spat, as she pushed her way back up.

She was wobbly but determined as she pushed herself to her feet.

"St. Augustina, wait," St. Benedict said, surging forward to come between her and the man she was aiming for. "He's here to help us. Wait. Wait!" Even in her weakened state, her augmentations reinforced her joints against the other Saint's weight and strength, sliding him back several feet along the floor, slowing but not stopping her. Over his shoulder, she saw the rattish face of Calvin as the cowardly man took a frightened step back.

"If it hadn't been for you two, I could have gotten everyone out of there alive! Dave, Phil... Brenda died in my arms! Because of you!"

"St. Augustina," St. Rachel joined them, coming behind to loop her arms through St. Augustina's armpits, either to help hold her back or hold her up, it was hard to tell. The world was swirling outside of her focus. "St. Auggie, it's over. Whatever deal or issues you two had in the past, it's not important right now. What's important..."

"Don't call me St. Auggie." St. Augustina tried to pull away, but it proved too hard to maintain her balance and she had to grab St. Benedict's shoulders to stabilize. "Where is he? What did you all do with the Poh?"

"We returned him to where he belonged," Lady Ursula said.

"Where's that?" St. Augustina demanded, but she noticed right away how Calvin's jaw thrust out indignantly. "You have it?" She narrowed her eyes even further at him. "How? Where is it?" She struggled against St. Benedict again, but her knees were becoming water around the reinforcement that still relied on her motor skills to function. "Get out of my way. It's not too late. I can still go back."

She tried once more to move toward Calvin and instead fell to her hands and knees, awkwardly, since the Saints near her were still trying to help keep her up.

Lacking any success in moving toward him, she glared up at Calvin. She could tell that he had changed. Not so much him personally; he was still a slimy little rat who would almost be handsome if it wasn't for the contemptuous sneer that was as much a part of his look as the blond hair on his head. This biggest change was in his clothes. When she had last seen him, and in fact, every memory she had ever had of him, he had been dressed in the kind of suit that would have looked perfect as an extra in a gangster movie.

Now, he wore jeans and a dark hoody. He also had boots on that went up to his knees, the leather tooled and elegant and out of sync with the casual wear, he otherwise sported. His hair was longer, too, not overly slicked back but tousled like he had gotten out of bed. It revealed how soft it was naturally. Around his neck hung a black amulet, which he fingered nervously with one hand.

She remembered.

It was much like the amulet the well-dressed woman had given him that was supposed to allow a mortal man to wield the power of the Oberon. True, the men who used it often died shortly after, but at the time, it had been a tactical move. Surprisingly, Calvin was still alive and using that power. It had to be how he was controlling the Poh. Blinking, she was also surprised to realize she remembered everything that had happened in the Poh's dreams.

"You have to give it back to me, the creature. You have to put me back to sleep," she said to the man with all the leverage, whose blond eyebrows lifted in surprise. The room was spinning again, "...promise."

"What is she talking about?" St. Rachel asked, exchanging a glance with St. Benedict, then spreading that glance to the other people in the room. "Calvin, what is she talking about?"

"Hell if I know. Didn't you all say she was crazy?!" Calvin shouted, backing even further away from the Saints.

"St. Augustina, it's been months, all right? A lot's changed since then; slow down and let us explain everything," St. Benedict said.

"I know!" St. Augustina shouted. "And you don't have a fucking clue what you've done! You're all too damn busy trying to be the big damn hero to realize..." Instead of finishing, she swallowed down the bile rising in her throat. It was happening. She was running out of time. "That thing and I had a deal. If you don't hurry, then I'm dead, anyway."

"I..." Calvin blinked at her, then a change came over his features. The sneer disappeared, showing how handsome he really was, almost beautiful. Then he turned his head to glance at Lady Ursula, who had come to stand beside him. A rack of antlers moved with him.

It was so incongruous with her expectations, that St. Augustina ceased struggling to stare wide-eyed at it. Why hadn't she noticed them earlier? She realized that he'd *had* antlers the entire time, but she simply hadn't registered it. Was delusion a part of dying? She couldn't rule it out.

He continued murmuring to himself. "I see. Yes. She is correct. The Poh, who was apart from The Oberon, offered to save the woman in exchange for possessing her... from certain death to the slow demise of its consumption of her mind and soul." His voice deepened and flowed more easily, still with a Chicago lilt but one inherently soothing to St. Augustina's ears, like the Poh's had been. Then he squatted down in front of St. Augustina, and her heart kicked up another notch. His eyes were the brightest blue, twinkling like jewels with their own internal light. She felt the same as when the Poh had looked at her with its blood-red eyes, entranced and intimidated all at once. The slight sneer of his lips was purely Calvin.

CHAPTER 9

"What would drive you to commit such a desperate act, child?" Lady Ursula asked gently.

St. Augustina looked up at her, but she couldn't be angry at this woman. It would be too much like shouting at her own mother.

"I lost my entire team. I failed my mission, and now, it's been months since I reported back. They are killing me."

"If they find you," Lady Ursula said, her eyebrows pinching together. "Whoever *they* are, and I can assure you *they* will not reach you here."

"No. I'm *dying*. Right now..." It was getting harder to breathe. "They can reach us anywhere," St. Augustina said. "It's magic. We've got no protection from that."

That set Lady Ursula back on her heels a bit. "Magic? What magic?" Her eyes began to rove over St. Augustina's body as if she could see it, then her eyes glazed over, flashing an orange-tinged white light that obscured her pupils and irises completely.

"She means her Saint Box," St. Rachel said, "And she's right. I thought of it before, when St. Benedict called me here, but then I dismissed the idea since we had more urgent issues to deal with. But it's standard procedure when controlling a Saint. If she's been captured or simply disappeared, they would terminate her using the Saint Box to safeguard themselves from her spilling their secrets or being somehow used against them."

"Including, nuking the technology within her," St. Benedict added.

"Yes, I see." Lady Ursula's opaque eyes drifted over to St. Augustina's right to St. Benedict, who squatted next to her. Her turning head was the only indication of where she was looking. "But they couldn't destroy you while the Poh possessed you. *Its* magic, the magic of the Oberon, would be strong enough to shield her from this type of enslavement magic," Lady Ursula said, bringing her knowledge to the conversation. "Fortunately, and unfortunately, I recognize this."

With one long, orange-enameled fingernail, Lady Ursula slipped out the chain from around St. Benedict's neck, pulling it free from under the collar of his button-up shirt. The chain itself was beautiful, the links doubled to create extra strength. Hanging from it was a silver box, much like St. Augustina's had been, carved with runes on each side. His was smaller than St. Augustina's and squarer, whereas hers had been rectangular.

The dying Saint's eyes went wide at the sight of it.

"You... you have your box?" she whispered, shocked. Unbidden, her fingers stretched out toward it with the hesitant reverence of a true believer gazing upon a long-sought-after holy relic.

Before she could, his own long fingers wrapped around it protectively, shielding it from her. "Yes," he whispered, matching her tone.

St. Rachel pulled hers free from her sweater as well, her chain more delicate with its single links, her box as long as one of her fingers.

"How... how did you get them back?" St. Augustina asked, forcing her voice to gain strength.

"We took them back," St. Benedict said.

"But... who is your master? Without a master, how are the boxes not killing you?" St. Augustina's fingers curled into fists. She couldn't name what she was feeling, but it trembled within her, in the middle of the whirlpool trying to pull her under. Was it hope?

"We have a master," St. Rachel said. "He helped us get our boxes back, and we chose him to be our master when we couldn't find a way to break the magic."

"A powerful wizard tried, but she couldn't break them. She said no one could, so we manipulated the magic to do what we wanted. It's not freedom, but it is better than nothing," St. Benedict explained, saying the words like they were still poison in his mouth.

St. Augustina's hand scraped across her throat, where the Saint Box had been in the dream, where the Poh had made her believe it had been. She wanted it now. She wanted it more than anything. Choice. The ultimate expression of freedom. The ache for it went deeper than anything she had ever felt for a lover, harsher than the pain of missing her parents, more heart-breaking than anyone's betrayal.

But it was too late. She was already dying. Collapsing to the ground, St. Augustina could only look up at the shocked faces above her. She could see them shouting but could no longer hear it, no longer feel their hands. This was it. It was finally over, but she still didn't want to go. A tear leaked from the side of her eye as she blinked one last time.

"I keep my oath," Calvin said with the Poh's voice, and he grabbed St. Augustina's hand before anyone else could react. Her whole body seized up, and she was gone again into the darkness, his voice the only one she could hear.

Immediately, her senses returned. But she was falling. Crashing back into blackness. She realized she was going back into the diner. The booth formed up around her, the neon casting its light while the auto-waitress filled up her cup again.

"You are mine."

"No! No, I'm not," St. Augustina resisted. She could feel it happening, feel her starting to forget, but something deeper inside herself couldn't do it again. "No, you can't."

"Why?"

There on the table before her was the cookie jar, exactly where she had left it, and beside that, her Saint Box, her mother's dog tags snug inside.

"I can be free!" There was a way. She knew that now, and even as every-thing else she knew about herself dissolved away, she held on to that thought. "I can be free. There is a way."

Like glass, the darkness cracked, and the diner fell away, breaking into chunks of reality. She floated in nothingness, the only light coming from the LED edging of her trench coat. The illogic of the mind would not yield to what was happening to her.

"I will keep you safe," the Poh as Calvin said.

But it wasn't enough anymore. "No," she said softly.

"Or you will die."

"No!"

"Then, you will survive."

"I don't want that anymore, either!" she screamed.

"Well, then make up your damned mind! I can't hold you like this forever. I got my own shit to take care of!"

The darkness cracked more, those pieces also falling away. Trees appeared around her. Warm and wet, the air smelled of loam and earth. Calvin stood before her, his larger hand still engulfing hers. The antlers were gone, replaced by white mist curling up over his head. The Poh's horned head covering the top half of his face obscured his face. His other hand slipped under the horse's head to rub his human eyes.

"Look, I'm sorry. I get that this is a stressful situation, but you have to make a choice."

She knew he was right. It was so absurd she couldn't help but chuckle. "I'm literally standing in the doorway between life and death."

Calvin half-shrugged. "Something like that. I mean, my understanding of all this is, it's a lot of metaphor, anyway. Magic realms, worlds within worlds within worlds, etc. I understand like every fifth thing with this whole Faerie King gig."

"You're a Faerie?" St. Augustina asked.

Again, the half-shrug. "Like I said, I only kind of understand it. And, I'm not supposed to call myself that. I'm the 'Oberon.' Only non-Faeries call me the Faerie King. I don't really get the difference, but what I do get is that we are in the in-between. Like it's in between me taking you back under, where you will survive, or me letting you wake up, in which, I guess, you're dying. I can hold you here... in this twilight state for... well, quite a while, but not forever. You need to make a choice. Up or down."

"To live or to die? Why are those always the only choices?" It was rhetorical, and Calvin had enough awareness apparently to understand that, so he remained silent.

Then she laughed. It sounded mad to her ears, bouncing with little manic echoes off the trees, but she couldn't help it. Maybe this was what going mad felt like.

"Idrina? What is it, Idrina?" Calvin asked, shouting a bit to cut through her laughter.

St. Augustina blinked. "Idrina. Yeah. That used to be my name. I used to hate it because it was so long. Who knew that was only going to get worse?"

"Look, I'm giving you a choice here…"

She felt so calm. It was as if she had never been more awake in her life.

"Yes, you are. Thank you. It's the only thing I've ever wanted in my whole life. And I always had it, didn't I?"

To her right, a figure appeared amongst the trees, the twilight world shaping itself to her thoughts. It was St. Cornelius as he had been when she last saw him.

Then she was back in the memory. She remembered her back pressed to the concrete wall she was sheltering behind, bullets flying around them. She had been terrified. They were pinned down, and every bullet was intended to kill her. St. Benedict was on the other side of the doorframe, shouting, trying to get her attention, to give her instructions, but she couldn't look away from St. Cornelius. He was strange, the look on his face so serene and incongruous with the surrounding chaos. He was simply standing there beside her. Then he straightened, setting his rifle down beside her and placing her hand on it. She thought he said, "In case you need it," before he moved past her and stepped into the doorway.

She couldn't remember screaming. She must have because it had been horrifying watching the bullets tear through a human body like that. St. Benedict had thrown out a hand to pull St. Cornelius out of the doorway, but a bullet skimmed over the skin of his forearm, not enough to incapacitate him, but enough to force his reflexes to recoil the arm out of danger.

The whole time, St. Cornelius's face had the same look of serenity as if what was happening to his body wasn't happening to him.

"You made a choice, didn't you?" St. Augustina asked him, both in the memory and in the moment, as her focus returned to the dream forest.

"There's always a choice," St. Cornelius said. "Not always a great one, but yes."

"I was afraid of your choice. I didn't want to make that one," St. Augustina.

"Good," he said, offering a small smile, "You aren't me. Make a different one."

"It's why you gave me your gun, isn't it? You knew I could fight. I could survive."

"In case you need it," he repeated.

"I did need it."

Another memory surfaced, and St. Augustina was back in that hallway, pushed out the door by St. Benedict. She remembered the sound of him locking it. When she banged on it, screaming for him to open it, it was like banging on a wall. He never turned to look at her, no matter how hard she screamed. His attention was firmly forward, staring at the metal cutter as it created the only escape out.

She believed she would die. There was no other choice. He had taken that choice away from her. Still, she pounded and pounded. Please look at me. Please save me. Please have mercy on me. Please, please, please, don't leave me with no choice, except to die.

"Except there was another choice," she said out loud, staring down the hallway as the angry shouting became louder. The enemy closing in. If they were going to kill her either way, what was she going to do?

"I chose to face it," she said calmly. "I had a weapon in case I needed it. And I did." She met her enemy head-on, racing to the end of the hallway to the doorway, separating her from her choice. Turning to step out, she filled the doorway, like St. Cornelius had. Only her enemy wasn't expecting it and many dropped in her first onslaught. Still, they kept coming.

And she had survived.

She had eventually escaped down a mail shoot. The drop would have broken her legs if she hadn't been augmented. And St. Benedict would have been a dead man if her Saint Box hadn't compelled her to stop.

"You are cursed with dark magic," Calvin said, bringing her back to the woods.

"I know this magic is evil," St. Augustina said dryly. She held up the fake Saint's Box, the one that looked so much like hers, wishing she could make herself drop it, but loathe to do so.

"I didn't say it was evil," he said, a little bit of his typical whine lacing through his voice. "In the right circumstances, this magic can be used to help people."

"Help people!" St. Augustina felt her blood boil. Instantly, she was back to when they first demonstrated how their Saint Boxes work. She had been the one they demonstrated it on, the only black woman in the room. All the other Saints stared in horror as the Deacon held her box, stood over her with a cruel smile, and told her not to breathe.

And she didn't.

She wanted to, badly, but her lungs wouldn't obey her. Something that had been so automatic her entire life, now couldn't even be done deliberately. The Deacon had gone on to explain in a leisurely way, that even their autonomic systems would obey the magic if their Masters commanded it. Just before she blacked out into starry nothingness, he chided her to breathe already.

She remembered clearly the sound of him laughing at her as she gulped painful breaths. "Don't worry. You're all too valuable for anyone to simply murder you in order to watch you die, even if it would be fun."

Calvin's eyes were strangely sympathetic when that particular memory faded back.

"Don't think I don't understand what kind of choice you've left me with here," she said.

"And what if it wasn't certain death?" a new voice asked.

Standing a few feet away, on the edge of the circle of trees, was Lady Ursula. Not the elegant older woman, but the younger one, dressed magnificently in vibrant oranges and yellows. Her eyes glowed with ethereal light. "I know this magic. The Oberon is right. It is a forbidden form of discipline except to those who need it most. It does not have to be certain death."

"How?" St. Augustina asked, warily. Wary of wanting to hope.

"You could retrieve your box," Lady Ursula asked.

The Saint shook her head. "I don't know where it is or who has it. The magic is killing me *now*. There is no time to look for it."

"Would you be able to ask your friends for help to find it for you?"

"Take it on faith that they'll expend resources, time, and their own lives to help me. No Saint would take that calculation. We're not that altruistic," she said with complete certainty.

"They came here to help you?" Lady Ursula questioned.

"Debts are not charity. He abandoned me in the vault. I would say this one is as paid as it can be."

Lady Ursula pursed her lips but did not try to contradict St. Augustina's claim. "I can see what they did, those that cast this curse upon you. Like I said, it is not the first time I've seen this sort of magic before, which is why it is mostly forbidden. It uses the subject's most beloved connection, something or someone they value more than anything, and infects it, using that as a way in through the defenses of the soul, bending them to another's will. To enslave them. To break this magic, the subject must completely forsake the connection, which can be a nigh impossible thing to do, since you cannot simply stop loving something because you choose to. But what they have done to you is even more sinister."

St. Augustina furrowed her brow. "What did they do?" she asked.

"Somehow, they've bound it into your augmentations, and this is the part I don't understand, since magic and technology do not mix, yet they can both exist in you without canceling each other out. I cannot undo one without removing the other, and I don't know where that would leave you."

"Just as dead or an equivalent vegetable, probably. So even if I wanted to... give away... my mother, I couldn't," St. Augustina said, her voice going soft. The idea of no longer feeling anything about her mother... she could see how such a thing was impossible. "Then, if I may cling to the small bit of hope here..." Her mind worked to form the thought. "I cannot choose to remove this curse from me, but I can choose who the curse binds me to?"

"Yes, it can be transferred. I believe that is a task I am equal to," Lady Ursula confirmed.

"If I could get ahold of my Saint Box before it kills me." St. Augustina lifted up the fake Saint Box, looking at it closely. She had only seen the real one a handful of times, and yet she had every curve and indention memorized.

Running her thumb over the top of the fake box, she focused on the sensation of dipping into the carved rune, something that looked like a fancy pi symbol, that had a little bit of roughness at the corner of the upper slash, where the tool that had carved it had pulled up. "If only this were real."

"Technically, it is real," Calvin said. "In this world."

"This is a dream?" St. Augustina cocked her head at him.

"Is it?" he said, smiling cockily.

"What is real here is real here, in this dream. What gets lost in the transition to the waking world is where magic comes in," Lady Ursula said. "To simplify a very complicated idea into the easiest explanation I can, magic takes what you dream and brings it into reality. You dream your Saint Box, that you have it, that you are complete with it. The Oberon's magic makes it real here, in the world he controls absolutely. You are sharing his dream world, and in that dream world, your Saint Box is real and the dream of someone else out there, that your Saint Box gives the holder of it the power to kill you, cannot touch you here in this realm."

"This is the simple explanation?" St. Augustina raised an eyebrow.

Lady Ursula smiled. "Like I said, it is complicated. Now, how Faerie magic works is different from how other magic works, but the underlying magic is the same principle. The Fae Royalty can sometimes bring such dreams into the waking world."

"Okay, she's making that sound… *waaaaay*…. easier than it is," Calvin said.

St. Augustina waved him off, her mind working at top speed. "The Poh and I had a deal, and now neither of us can fulfill it. Can I make another deal in its place?"

Calvin blew out a breath. "Yes. I'm going to say yes."

"Could I make this real?" St. Augustina said, holding up her Saint Box.

Calvin stared at it. "Maybe?"

"What do you need to try?"

CHAPTER 10

itting in the diner, looking out over the city, St. Augustina marveled at its beauty. She took in each billboard, each twist of neon as the work of art it truly was. She wondered where she had seen all of it to draw from to create this world, or if it was purely conjured fantasy. Sure, they were selling everything from diet pills to sex pills to the latest vacuum cleaner, yet there was silent poetry to the lights and figures moving through the madness and color. There was even more poetry to her sitting above it all, sipping hazelnut-flavored synth-coffee, nibbling on the sweet potato pie that tasted exactly like her great aunt's secret recipe. If only she knew the secret.

In the haven of the anonymous diner, she waited for her client.

No.

Shaking her head, she tried to focus. There was no client coming. She *was* waiting for someone, though. Her dream continued, and she had to work to not get swept away into it. He would be here soon enough.

The door tinkled as it opened inward, and she smiled.

"St. Benedict, have a seat," she said, offering a hand to the bench across from her.

With a playboy smile on his face, St. Benedict obliged her, sliding into the exact middle, before resting his hands on the table.

"Are you alright?" he asked. The first question out of his mouth. She decided not to ignore the significance of that. She needed that to tell him what she had decided. She owed him that much, at least.

"Yeah, I think so. What is it like on the outside, in the waking world?" she asked.

"So, you do remember who I am then? No more of this reset, forget-everything crap?" he asked. But then, St. Benedict was never suave when he was honest.

"No. I have all my memories, as long as I focus," she confirmed, before taking another long swallow of the delicious synth-coffee, so much like the real thing. Somehow knowing this was all a dream had made the synth-coffee taste better.

"I am so sorry that we weren't able to fully save you," St. Benedict said. He lifted his hat and ran his fingers through his hair in that strange habit he had when he was agitated. "I thought I was helping you."

"You did," she said, reaching across the table to squeeze his hand. "You helped me a lot."

"Then why doesn't it feel like it?" he asked, with a weak smile.

"It's not your fault," she said, going over her rehearsed answer as smoothly as if she had thought of it that moment. "You didn't create the Saint program, did you?"

"No." He nodded. "But I did buy into it, didn't I?"

"I think we all did," she agreed. The auto-waitress came by and silently refilled her cup, which meant she had to reach for the hazelnut creamer again to balance it out. The temperature was perfect on the first sip.

"I promise, we'll keep working on finding a solution," St. Benedict said.

It was as good of an opening as any.

"What? You'll do whatever it takes to save me?" She smiled over the rim of her cup. "Don't make promises you can't keep. It gets you in trouble."

He grinned. "Haven't you noticed? I like trouble."

"Well, would you?"

"Would I what?"

"Do whatever it took to save me?"

His head jerked at that. "I suppose. If I can do it."

She grinned herself. There it was. There was no such thing as Saint altruism. "Are you in love with me, St. Benedict? Is that why it matters so much to you?" she teased, setting him back at ease.

"I was pretty sure *you* were," he fired back, lifting his arm to rest on the back of the booth with a jovially arrogant air.

She laughed with a mouth full of synth-coffee, losing some back into the cup. He lifted his hands and mocked being insulted.

"Some people find me quite handsome," he declared.

"Some people didn't see you before they changed your face. You were pretty then," St. Augustina declared.

"Yeah, well, they don't know us, do they? We're Saints."

His eyes were so warm. She regarded them for a moment playing with the cup in her hands, reveling in the understanding passing between them. Not yet. She wasn't ready to ask him just yet. Needed to soften him up more. "I will get my Saint Box back one day."

"And you're going to ask St. Rachel and me to keep looking for it," he said, leaning forward to place his folded hands on the table. "That's what this is all leading up to, isn't it?"

She went on as if he hadn't just spoken. "You see, the reason I think you helped me is that you do, in fact, feel guilty for abandoning me to die in the vault. Now, I never saw your face, but that was why you couldn't bear to look at me, isn't it? You couldn't stand to watch me die."

"You didn't die," he said, deadly soft.

"No, I didn't. Kind of made it worse, didn't it?"

He went still a moment, carefully picking his words. "I'm glad you didn't." He stopped his next breath, licking his lips as he struggled.

"I want you to give me your Saint Box."

He sat there a moment, as if he wasn't sure what he had heard, his smile growing more fragile with each passing second. "Excuse me?"

"The Oberon believes he can create a temporary fix, a sort of false Saint Box using yours as the catalyst, to trick the magic into making this one…" She slipped the chain around her neck free so that the box rotated unencumbered before his sharp, green gaze. "Making it exist in the waking world."

"But what does that mean?" he asked flatly. "Use mine how?"

She let her chain drop, the box thumping lightly against her sternum. "Our hearts live in these boxes, right? Your heart will beat for the both of us until I find and reclaim my own."

He stared at her box a moment. "And if you don't?"

She thinned her lips. "It can't go on forever. I will release your box before it kills us both. But it won't come to that if it works."

He narrowed his eyes even more. "That's a lot of 'ifs.'"

St. Augustina didn't have an answer for that, so she didn't try to give one. Deliberately, she drained the rest of her cup, swallowing down the bitter at the bottom.

"I can't."

"You can't or you won't?"

"Fine, I won't, then. What you're asking for… you're wrong, I don't owe you my life. I've already given it to someone else. I can't offer it to you, not like that. I already risked too much to get you this far. I'm sorry."

She didn't say anything. She hadn't really expected a different answer.

He shifted in his seat. "We'll find your Saint Box. I promise. St. Rachel and I, we'll do whatever we can."

She didn't respond to that either, only kept looking at him with her blanked eyes, keeping his focus on her.

"Have you asked St. Rachel yet if she'd be willing to..."

"You know, I'm actually relieved it turned out this way," she said. Too late, St. Benedict detected the danger in her voice. He moved to scramble away, but she was already moving through the table like it wasn't there. Because it wasn't.

She grasped her hand around his throat. His own arm came up to try to counter her, but he hadn't sensed her neo-ninjas at all before they grabbed his limbs, holding him fast.

"This is my Dream, St. Benedict. Did you think you could walk into my mind and do whatever you wanted to me?"

"I tried to help you."

"You were only helping yourself. Everything you've ever done has been to help yourself."

Her neo-ninjas forced him to his knees, and she let go of his throat, slipping the chain around his neck between her fingers.

"No. Everything I've done has been for her," he growled.

"Including sacrificing me. Who said I was yours to sacrifice for your *her*?"

He dragged his head up, glaring at her from under the brim of his fedora, unable to answer her because he knew she was right. She didn't need to hear him say it. They both understood. They were both Saints.

"Well, get on with it then," he growled.

Calvin ghosted in behind her, his rack of antlers towering over their heads. Though she did not look at him, she knew what he looked like in the logic of dreams.

St. Benedict's glare drifted over her shoulder. "Oh, you must be loving this."

"I'm going to admit... yeah, a little bit," Calvin answered.

St. Benedict smiled his sharp, wicked smile. "Say hello to your wife for me."

She sensed an angry stiffening coming from the Faerie King. "Take his Saint Box in your hand," Calvin instructed. Gripping it tight at the end of its chain, the box was still warm from being against his skin. Her salvation.

Calvin's hand cupped her shoulder, and she had to resist the urge to pull away from his touch. It was electrical and cold, like the feel of the Poh's magic when it had pulled her into the world of dreams. Maybe that was just how magic was.

Without needing to be told, she slipped the dream Saint Box into her other hand, willing it to be real.

St. Benedict's back arched, air hissing in through his teeth. There was a flash, and St. Augustina realized she was awake. Her eyes had been open the whole time, but she knew that now she was really awake.

Like in the dream, St. Benedict knelt before her. Two men she did not recognize had replaced her neo-ninjas, their ink-black skin as startling as the bright white skulls covering their faces. It was no more than an instant before her vision flashed again.

She saw a woman, young and pretty, with laughing eyes. She reached out to cup St. Augustina's cheek.

"I love you," she said, and then she too was gone.

"What was that?" St. Augustina asked, her heart pounding loudly.

"What he holds in the box," the Oberon said. "It is almost over." Wind blew around them. Before her, St. Benedict's augmented eyes glowed blue. Holograms began flashing around him, screens that looked like a mix of computer code and runes.

"Do you want this?" the Oberon's voice spoke calmly and clearly despite the chaos surrounding them. He had come around to face St. Augustina, his crystal eyes wise and alien at the same time.

"Yes," St. Augustina said, unflinching as she lowered her chin, driving her focus into her glowing fingers. She felt her own augmentation activate, the world glowing yellow for a moment, then her left eye changed, and the light was blue.

"Choose your master."

That caught St. Augustina off guard. She hadn't put any thought into that, needing to choose the one who would still have power over her. Who did she wish to serve?

As if by the pull of a magnet, she was drawn toward Lady Ursula, who was watching the proceedings impassively to the side.

It was so obvious.

As if she had already asked the question, Lady Ursula nodded her head. "I would be honored."

St. Augustina moved toward her, releasing St. Benedict's Saint Box while holding out her own toward the Lady. With great solemnity, Lady Ursula took it, then unfolded the chain and clasped it around her new Saint's neck.

With that, it was over. All light died and then returned to passive candlelight. She heard St. Benedict gasping for breath, but she felt... fine. Normal. Alive.

"It's working," she sighed in relief as if she hadn't really believed it would. Then, she turned to Lady Ursula. "I'm awake?"

The Lady smiled warmly at her. "Yes, child. I'd say more awake than most of us, right now."

St. Augustina plucked up the new Saint Box resting against her chest. It wasn't her original one, she knew it wouldn't be, but she was surprised to see the shape of the old one only wrought in blackness. In fact, it was a reversal of the normal Saint Boxes. The body of it was blackened, and the runes inscribed into the surfaces winked silver. Gently she shook it. There was no clink inside. It was empty. Of course, it was. Her mother's dog tags were still housed within the old one.

"Thank you," she said softly to her new Master.

"What have you done to him?!" St. Rachel's voice was shrill as it cut through the air. Looking to the door, St. Augustina saw the beautiful woman standing there. She had not cared where St. Rachel had been the whole time she was conducting her operation against St. Benedict, that detail had been out of her control being asleep. She had simply trusted that the third Saint had been properly distracted.

She had trusted. What an interesting thought.

St. Rachel pushed past the monochrome men, the men of black and white who guarded the door. The two who had been holding St. Benedict had let him drop to the ground, where he knelt still, breathing hard. As St. Rachel grabbed him, though, he held up his hand, wincing like he had a headache.

"I'm fine, I'm fine. Go easy." He pushed himself back to his feet, readjusting his shirt as he got himself together. St. Rachel dropped her hands uselessly, before folding them across her chest as she too gathered up her care, concern, and any other vulnerable emotions tucked them back into their boxes inside herself. Two Saints re-armoring themselves.

"What did she do to you?" St. Rachel asked again coolly, this time directing her eyes to St. Augustina.

"I'm not sure. I can run a diagnostic when we get back." He reset his fedora, then turned to St. Augustina, his green-blue eyes looking through her. She met them full-on, not flinching from what she had done.

St. Rachel's eyes were a pair of blue needles. "Let's get out of here. Or if you're going to stay, I'll just go."

"No, I'll escort you out," he said genially.

"Don't think I need another knife in the back," she replied.

"We are Saints after all," St. Benedict said, jovially. "I wouldn't trust me with a knife, either."

While they seemed to be talking to each other, the entire exchange was done while still looking at St. Augustina, but she only met their thinly veiled innuendos with silence. St. Benedict nodded his head in a polite goodbye, his smile poisonous. "Lady Ursula."

"I trust you will be reporting these events to your Master?" Lady Ursula said with a politician's grace.

"Well, that would involve explaining where I've been disappearing to these last few months." He turned and the monochrome men parted. He offered his arm to St. Rachel, who ignored it to walk out on her own. He didn't comment on it, only slipped his hands into his pockets and followed after her.

"Do you regret it?" Lady Ursula asked as soon as the other Saints were gone.

"We are Saints," St. Augustina said, looking out the door as if she could still see them. In a way, she would always be looking. "There is no loyalty, no love, no trust between us. There can't be if we want to survive. Only prices to be paid later."

St. Augustina stared down at the city below, grey and dull in the diffused sunlight of the winter day. Snow covered everywhere that hadn't been shoveled and shuffled back into piles on the curbs or between cars. People in mostly dark coats moved about their business, but not in too much of a hurry to escape the wind, so it probably wasn't too cold out there.

"It's not much of a view today," Lady Ursula's voice said from the desk, positioned perpendicular to the window. "They say it might snow again. You'll have to come back when it's bright and clear. You can usually see the lake from here. Pretty gray and dismal right now."

"I don't mind it. It's been ages since I last saw any sort of daylight," St. Augustina said, not tearing her eyes away from the view. "It was also summer then. It's almost like I've traveled to another country."

"There and back again?" Lady Ursula said, sounding amused.

"I suppose so," St. Augustina agreed, turning back into the room.

The office was lovely, even in the dull light. Lamps were on, instead of harsh fluorescents, which made it feel warmer than a heater would have. It was filled with greenery, large leafy plants surrounded every lamp. It was akin to a greenhouse if it wasn't for the antique walnut shelves filled with books and the large walnut desk covered with bizarre knickknacks St. Augustina assumed were for the working of magic. There were also two dark leather chairs positioned in front of the desk, and it was one of these that St. Augustina claimed as hers.

"Something else I would like to understand," St. Augustina began as she settled into the chair.

"Please," Lady Ursula incited, "any answers I can provide, I shall."

St. Augustina took a moment to phrase her question. "When we were... at the auction..." She sighed, the question was bigger than that. "Well, all of it. Was all of it necessary?"

CHAPTER 10

"How I understand it, your mind had laid traps to keep you in the Poh's power. Fae are masters of illusion and truck in metaphor. The Poh fed your dreams with its magic to create a truly fantastical world. It had its own rules that you believed completely. We had to follow your rules. Now we know why."

"We do?"

"You were exactly where you wanted to be. Seeing exactly what you expected to see. Your ego had as much control over what was happening as a child does a car when it tries to steer from the passenger seat with its toy steering wheel. Most of the functions of life have nothing to do with your ego at all."

At that disconcerting thought, St. Augustina furrowed her eyebrows. "Then... why.... the mistress, you offered to bid on her, but she wasn't real. What was the point of that?"

"Ah, yes. Well, I got curious. I wanted to know what you would do."

"It almost cost us St. Benedict... except... and what would have happened to him if it was simply a dream?"

"Well, that's where things got messy. He was 'jacked' into your computer bits, trying to get you to activate some kind of emergency program. And when your protection protocols activated, we couldn't wake him up again either. At that point, St. Rachel went into you both, in the hopes that she could get you to finish unlocking your emergency program, which you designed to look like a cookie jar. Unlocking that allowed you to reboot the system while at the same time the Oberon and I called the Poh out of you, returning it to the Oberon."

St. Augustina stared at her, and the lady blushed. "I hope that made sense. I don't entirely understand what all your technological words mean exactly.

St. Augustina nodded. "It made enough sense, thank you."

Silently, she regarded the blood-red geode Lady Ursula had sitting on a leather placemat before the woman of magic.

"This is the last one," Lady Ursula said, tapping it with an enameled finger. "Dream geodes. A very powerful tool that can call a soul back from a dream. Among other uses."

"And once those were gone, you were going to give up on me?" St. Augustina asked.

"Not for an instant. But it may have been difficult to obtain more as easily as I obtained these." She gestured to the small pile of ashy geodes, each looking like they had been burned out, which was impossible since crystal didn't burn. As far as St. Augustina knew.

"Were they... costly?" St. Augustina asked, steepling her fingers.

"It doesn't matter," the Lady said.

"Which means they were." The Saint stared at the geode. "Why did you do this for me? You don't know me. I'm nobody to you."

"Sometimes, it is reward enough to bring a lost child home."

St. Augustina stood abruptly and went back to the window.

"You don't like that answer?" Lady Ursula said to her back.

"No." St. Augustina continued to stare out the window, but instead of studying the view, she looked at her augmented eyes being reflected back at her in the glass. One eye yellow, one eye glowing blue.

"Then, what answer would please you?" There was a clinking sound, and St. Augustina glanced back to see Lady Ursula preparing two cups from a fancy coffee set.

"I don't know... Give me a bill for services rendered. I'm used to being blackmailed into doing some work quid-pro-quo-like. Something trans-actional. But you're saying you had no idea what I was when you started to help me?"

"I understood you were augmented, and it was interfering with what help we could give you. That was when I took a chance and asked St. Benedict for assistance."

"I suppose it worked out well for you then. I may have been a costly investment, but now you have an invaluable asset."

"You weren't an investment, Idrina."

"You shouldn't call me Idrina," St. Augustina said, then immediately regretted. She shouldn't be itchy at hearing her own true name. "Though... you can call me whatever you like. You're my Master now, after all."

"St. Augustina," Lady Ursula obliged gently, "I was happy to help you. Whether you wish to believe it or not."

"Like I said, I would be more comfortable if you presented me with a bill, or a list of twelve impossible tasks."

"Honestly, I don't know what I could ask for of someone like you." Lady Ursula offered her a cup and saucer, which the Saint diplomatically took.

"Oh, believe me. I'm very useful."

"Alright, then, switch places with me, hypothetically. If you were me, what would I need from you?"

St. Augustina arched an eyebrow at the older woman, who only con-tinued to serenely smile as if she were a college professor having a delightful conversation with a promising student while she sipped her elegant coffee. St. Augustina took a polite sip that stopped her in her tracks.

"Hazelnut?" she asked, looking at the older woman.

"I was paying attention. In fact..." The older woman plucked a nut from a bowl of them sitting beside the coffee set and handed it to St. Augustina.

The Saint hesitated a moment, then took a nibble. Her eyebrows shot up as the familiar and new flavor burst in her mouth. "Uh. So that's what it actually tastes like."

Lady Ursula smiled over her cup, and at that moment, St. Augustina could see the mischievous teeny-bopper hiding in her features.

The Saint took another sip of the tea, collecting her thoughts. "I... first off, you do realize that your community is vulnerable. I mean, if I was to do a consultative assessment, the Magic Guild is not competing in any meaningful way with the fast-changing world out there." She nodded at the street below.

"We are aware," Lady Ursula conceded.

"No, I don't think you really are aware of just how bad it is," St. Augustina continued. "I have seen several analytics of the socioeconomic impact of the failure of the Magic Guild altogether. Your people are barely navigating this new technologically based world anymore. You've lost your competitive edge, your voice in government has been marginalized to a whisper, and soon, it'll be gone altogether, and the magical communities you represent won't have anyone anymore. I would... I would help with that."

"You would?" Now it was Lady Ursula's turn to arch an eyebrow. "How?"

"What you need is a consultant. Someone who can build a corporate support team. Lawyers who understand magical law and corporate law. Or maybe some that know one and other lawyers that know the other and they can work together to navigate it. You'd also need logistics advocates, to help navigate the bureaucracies. And you need to start getting your enrollment back up. You're hemorrhaging funds. I've seen the data, and more and more magically Talented people are being shanghaied into corporations with no real options to break out of their contracts and work where they choose. We'd need to make it possible to bring them back under your roof."

"Seems like a tall order."

"It would be the bare minimum, just to get started. I could triple that list. You're a drowning ship and don't even seem to know it."

"And you could be that person for us? Be our corporate advocate?"

"Not exactly. I'm a team builder. It's what I'm good at. I could start it, but what you would really want from me are the skills I've acquired for the 'not technically legal' activities. I am a Saint. I can make things happen that others can't, using whatever means necessary, and get away with it. It's what the designation means."

"In other words, you create miracles?" Lady Ursula sounded amused, but St. Augustina did not take offense at it.

"If that's what you wanna call 'em," she replied.

"And what kind of not-technically-legal activities do you imagine those of us in the magic community get up to?" Lady Ursula said with an arched eyebrow.

"I don't know exactly, I'd have to find out. But it isn't hard to imagine when corporate police are taking the law into their own hands. And their owners are working hard to make even having magic a crime onto itself. Just existing could soon be a crime."

"That would never happen," Lady Ursula said.

"Are you so sure about that?"

The two women regarded each other, and St. Augustina let the weight of those words settle in before saying, "You are going to need someone to be able to cheat a system that was never designed to work, to even have a chance of surviving. That is where I would come in."

"Would you really want to do that? Continue being a Saint, as you call it, but for us? For the benefit of the magic community?"

"Why are you asking me? I told you, you have only to order it."

"Why would you want me to do that?"

"Because if you don't, I won't do any of it. Why would I? There's no benefit in it for me. Right now, what would benefit *me* would be to solve this!" She fished out the black chain and the black box hanging from it. "I'm on borrowed time. This would be my entire focus."

"Maybe it should be. As you said, you are sharing his life," Lady Ursula's voice dropped, adding, "and he is sharing your death."

A bell sounded, coming from nowhere when a disembodied voice declared, "Your afternoon appointment has arrived."

"Thank you," Lady Ursula said to the air. St. Augustina moved to leave, though where to she wasn't sure, when Lady Ursula held up a hand for her to wait. "Nothing needs to be decided today. I am working to make arrangements for you, get you set up with money and a place to live, that kind of thing, since you are now my responsibility. So until then, why don't you talk all this over and let me know what you decide."

St. Augustina furrowed her brow. "Talk it over?"

"Yes. I imagine you have much to discuss." Lady Ursula gestured to the door, and it opened of its own accord.

Standing in the doorway with a look of surprise at the self-opening door, was a shorter, older woman, her hand still outstretched to grasp a door handle that was no longer there. Blinking, the woman took a step forward, her grey dreadlocks pulled back into a neat bun. She was dressed in a nice suit, with a soft, pink-striped scarf around her neck. Her dark eyes looked about the room a moment until they fell on the two women staring at her. A smile of greeting began to cross her face as she entered further into the room. Then it stopped as recognition filled her eyes, growing wider with shock.

"Idrina?" she asked as if she was unable to believe her own eyes.

"Mom?" St. Augustina's voice broke, her own tears already pouring down her cheeks unheeded. It was really her. She was really here. The Saint crumbled, becoming that teenage girl who had been stolen off the street all those years ago.

"Oh, my Lord!" her mother cried, and St. Augustina... Idrina... was across the room, which disappeared from her perception. Instead, there were only hugs and tears and kisses, embarrassing, beloved nicknames, and so many words, so much love.

CHAPTER 10

"I'm sorry, Mom, I'm sorry. I should have listened to you. I'm so sorry I sassed back, I'm so sorry," Idrina said, in an incoherent babble, all the things she had rehearsed a million times.

"They said you was gone forever. They said no way you were still out there, but I knew. Oh God above, I just knew, He hadn't taken my baby away from me. Not yet! Not just yet," her mother declared, squeezing her cheeks too hard as she looked into Idrina's reddened, wet eyes. "My girl. My brave warrior."

"I'm not brave, Mom. I'm not, I'm not," and she was in her mother's arms again, even though the woman was so much shorter than her. Even though she was ruining the pink scarf, it didn't matter. They stayed like that for ages.

When, at last, she came up for air, her mother moved to Lady Ursula, whose eyes were wet, too, in spite of the smile across her face.

"Thank you! Oh Lord, thank you for bringing my baby back to me."

Lady Ursula returned the hug before she clasped hands with Idrina's mother. "Sometimes, it is enough to bring a lost child home."

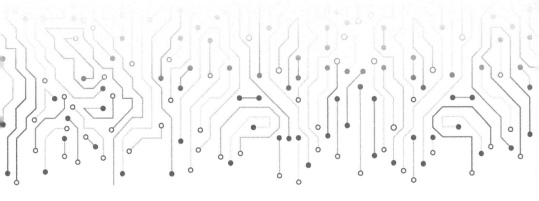

EPILOGUE

St. Benedict shifted back against the wall, barely able to move his legs a step further. He was safe, standing in the hallway outside Malachi's office. If St. Benedict were ever going to say he had a friend in this world, it would be Malachi. Too bad he couldn't say that.

For one thing, friends shared secrets or at least truths about themselves with each other. Not that there was anything Malachi hadn't told him whenever he did, and often when he didn't, ask. The friendship was one-sided, and because of that, St. Benedict felt honor-bound to never ask anything of the tech unless he absolutely needed it.

And even when he absolutely needed it, it could sometimes be hard.

So, the Saint stood there in the stillness of the nondescript gray hallway, pressing his aching skull against his palms, willing it to stop. He had told St. Rachel he was fine and was shocked when she accepted the lie. Maybe she was too tired, as well. He had asked too much of her as well.

"What the hell is the matter with you?" a smooth, rumbling voice asked.

St. Benedict gritted his teeth, but his training kept him from jumping at the sound. He never did completely relax.

"Long night, sir," he said to Maxamillion as his boss, and the designated owner of his Saint Box came down the hall, letting the metal door that separated them from the larger room of the underground facility clang closed behind him.

Elegantly dressed, as usual, in a dark chocolate, three-piece suit, his boss came up beside him folding his arms under, waiting for a better answer.

St. Benedict just offered him his usual placid smile.

"Anything you want to tell me? You've been disappearing rather a lot lately and don't think for a second that I believe you've taken up bowling or pottery or something a normal person would find relaxing."

And there it was. The moment St. Benedict had been thinking about since leaving Lady Ursula's. What was he going to do now?

He felt the burning sensation still in the back of his brain. The throbbing in his knees as St. Augustina had forced him to the ground. The sting of her betrayal.

He owed her nothing now. Dammit, he had been trying to save her life. And now the Magic Guild had a powerful new weapon, and Maxamillion's own weapon was compromised. Without his knowing, the power dynamic had shifted to jeopardize, or at the very least change, the deal that Maxamillion was trying to strike with the Magic Guild. If St. Benedict didn't say something to him, then St. Rachel would eventually. Oh, what kind of trouble would St. Benedict be in then? The kind he didn't have a recourse to deal with.

At least if he confessed now, to what he had been up to, then something could be done. Didn't he owe it to Maxamillion? Owe him something like loyalty?

Eh, fuck it.

"Nothing I want to tell you, but if you order me to, I will," St. Benedict said diplomatically, folding his own arms across his chest.

Maxamillion sucked his teeth before blowing his breath out, letting his arms drop. "I'm not out to get you, you know."

The response surprised the Saint, but he went with where karma pointed. "No, but you have your priorities, sir. I'm not going to do anything that will jeopardize what you're trying to accomplish. I promise," St. Benedict said sincerely.

White teeth smiled back at the Saint, enviably perfect. The best that money could buy. Maxamillion, for all his secret machinations for the betterment of mankind, had definitely kept the best for himself in all their endeavors, framing each as a reinvestment into the "silent war" effort. St. Benedict didn't blame him for it, or really think him a hypocrite, but considered him human. A black kid from the streets becomes a prince of La Salle St. Financial District. What else did anyone who was watching think was going to happen? Altruism was often the first casualty when a human being started getting used to actual money and actual power. All it meant was St. Benedict knew he couldn't trust that smile. Ever.

It was nice to know where he stood with his boss.

"I'm just going to head in with Malachi and do a quick diagnostic run," St. Benedict assured, making a show of letting his guard down a little, to set

Maxamillion more at ease. "I don't think anything's wrong other than I'm really burned out, but St. Rachel is all over me to be sure."

"She worries. And she's right to," Maxamillion said, his eyes already calculating. "You know what, I think I can shift some things off you for now. We're at a bit of a standstill with the Faerie Court, while they're dealing with their internal politics, as they are."

"Yeah, new kings will do that," St. Benedict quipped, trying not to think about Calvin or anything related to him, so it wouldn't appear on his face.

"Yes. So, take the rest of the week. Come back on duty on Monday."

"A vacation? Me?" St. Benedict feigned shock, resting his fingertips on his chest effeminately. "Why I do declare, that is most generous of ya, sir."

To his credit, Maxamillion didn't roll his eyes, but St. Benedict could see it was heavily implied, and that was enough for him.

"Thank you, sir," he responded normally.

"Don't leave Chicago or nothing... anything," the Prince of La Salle St. corrected, "in case an emergency pops up, but there are plenty of staycation options available. Have you seen Hamilton yet?"

"Are you offering me tickets?"

Thankfully, Malachi came out of his office at that moment, saving St. Benedict from having to make any further small talk with Maxamillion about his "staycation" options.

"Hey, St. Ben. You look like crap," Malachi said as cheerfully as always.

"Yeah, it happens," St. Benedict responded, feeling solid enough on his feet to not fall over if he pushed away from the wall. "Got a minute to check under the hood?" He tapped a finger against his temple.

"Yeah, sure, come on into my laboratory, *mwahaha*," Malachi added as he steepled his fingers, tapping them together in a repeating cascade to underscore his "evil scientist" laugh. "And you?" the tech continued in his persona, directing the question to his boss. "Is there anything I can do for you, milord?"

"Stop acting like a damned fool and get your ass back to work," Maxamillion said with zero mirth, which in itself was funny as Malachi instantly dropped his hands, to put them instead behind his back like he was ten and not twenty-something.

"Sorry, sir," Malachi actually said, and Maxamillion gave him warning eyes for good measure before marching back the way he came, whatever he had come to do apparently forgotten.

As soon as the door clanged shut, Malachi let out a whooping breath. "Geez, Louise. One of these days, I tell you. One of these days... I don't know what he's going to do, but I tell you I am genuinely afraid of whatever it will be."

"Geez Louise?" St. Benedict grinned.

"Yeah, you know, the mother of Holy Cripes, the son of Gosh?" Malachi turned to walk back into his office as the two men shared the chuckle.

"Hey, Mal," St. Benedict called, stopping him instead of following.

"Yeah, St. Ben?" Malachi lifted an eyebrow at his friend. It was so innocent and trusting, that St. Benedict almost lost his nerve.

"Do you...?" He swallowed once. "Do you think I'm a good man?"

Malachi stared unblinkingly at the question. Then lifted his hand flat and waved it back and forth like a ship on a choppy sea. "Eh?"

The smile returned to St. Benedict's face. "Yeah, that's what I thought." And he pushed off to go into the office ahead of Malachi.

"I mean, you're all right, as far as good guys go, but... you know, I would definitely say you're more anti-hero than actual hero.

"Okay, thanks, Mal."

"Or rather, how about chaotic neutral? I think that would be far more precise."

"You're making me regret asking."

AUTHOR BIO

Megan Mackie is a Chicago writer. With her smashing success with her inaugural, Amazon bestselling book, The Finder of the Lucky Devil, she is now the author of The Lucky Devil series, the Dead World series, and the Working Mask series, with other books coming out soon. She has become a personality at many cons, recognizable by her iconic leather hat and engaging smile.

Outside of her own series, she is a contributing writer for the RPGs with Onyx Path Publishing and Apotheosis Studios. Outside of writing, she likes to play games: board games, RPGs, and video games. She has a regular Pathfinder group that is working its way through Rapanthuk. She lives in Chicago with her husband and children, two dogs, two cats, and her mother in the apartment upstairs.

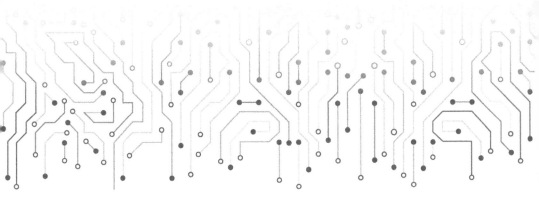

DEVIL DISCUSSION QUESTIONS

1. What images or ideas does the setting of Digital City invoke?

2. Who did you think the Orange Lady was at first? How did that evolve as the book went on?

3. How far off does the world of Digital City feel or seem from our current world?

4. What did you think was happening when St. Augustina woke up in the diner over and over again?

5. Does your perception of St. Rachel change in this book, compared to other stories in the same world where she is featured? How is she the same?

6. Even if most of the book took place in St. Augustina's mind, was she right to try to save the courtesan? Why or why not?

7. Though there was no love interest in this story, how was the story about love?

8. Who were you most surprised to see appear in this story?

9. Did St. Augustina do the right thing by the end? Was there a right answer she didn't take?

10. Where do you see St. Augustina's journey going from here?

More books from
4 Horsemen Publications

Paranormal & Urban Fantasy

Amanda Fasciano
Waking Up Dead
Dead Vessel

Beau Lake
The Beast Beside Me
The Beast Within Me
Taming the Beast: Novella
The Beast After Me
Charming the Beast: Novella
The Beast Like Me
An Eye for Emeralds
Swimming in Sapphires
Pining for Pearls

Chelsea Burton Dunn
By Moonlight

J.M. Paquette
Call Me Forth
Invite Me In
Keep Me Close

Jessica Salina
Not My Time

Kait Disney-Leugers
Antique Magic

Lyra R. Saenz
Prelude
Falsetto in the Woods: Novella
Ragtime Swing
Sonata
Song of the Sea
The Devil's Trill
Bercuese
To Heal a Songbird
Ghost March
Nocturne

Megan Mackie
The Saint of Liars
The Devil's Day
The Finder of the Lucky Devil

Paige Lavoie
I'm in Love with Mothman

Robert J. Lewis
Shadow Guardian and the Three Bears

Valerie Willis
Cedric: The Demonic Knight
Romasanta: Father of Werewolves
The Oracle: Keeper of the Gaea's Gate
Artemis: Eye of Gaea
King Incubus: A New Reign

SciFi

**DISCOVER MORE AT
4HorsemenPublications.com**

Lightning Source UK Ltd.
Milton Keynes UK
UKHW040233210223
417160UK00032B/856/J